The Goat Killer 2

Clive Ward

This book is dedicated to all who have served in the armed forces and are dealing with the effects of PTSD on a daily basis

By Clive Ward

The Unnamed Soldiers
Army Barmy
Bumpers & Bed Blocks
EndEx
EndEx 2 Uncut
EndEx 3
You Wouldn't Belize It
The Goat Killer
Homeless Free as a Bird
Trench 31

Writing with Elaine Ward

Half Day Closing
In Sympathy

I would like to thank my wife and family for their constant support. Big thanks go out to Lynn Lawson for her patience whilst editing the manuscript.

Chapter 1

The roads were still busy when Andy Ashford and his girlfriend, Sandra, arrived at the Derby City Centre bingo hall. It was the same routine every Friday. They would arrive just before quarter to six, buy their bingo tickets, find a seat and wait for the first session to begin. Their reason for arriving early was to take advantage of happy hour when all drinks were half price until quarter to seven when the bingo started.

Two hours later, at nine o'clock, it was all over and the mad rush to get out of the bingo hall began. People headed for the car park to get their cars or grab a taxi, most of them looking disappointed, apart from the lucky few who walked away with a few pounds more in their purse or wallet.

After the rush was over, Andy and Sandra continued their regular routine. Sandra pushed wheelchair bound Andy and headed to the chip shop on the opposite side of the road from the council house. It was always the same choice, fish cake, chips and mushy peas, with lots of salt and vinegar. They would usually make their way home to eat their supper, but tonight Sandra had other ideas.

'It's a nice evening Andy, shall we wander over to the River Gardens to eat it? At least we'll be left alone over there,' she said nervously.

'Yeah, why not.' Andy agreed.

The city centre of Derby on a Friday night, as with all other city centres, would get very crowded, mainly with young people heading for the clubs, bars and restaurants. It also had its fair share of anti-social behaviour, mostly fuelled by drug and alcohol problems and sometimes by people with mental health issues. Then of course every city has its beggars and down and outs, usually sitting in doorways, quietly asking for a few pounds as people walk by, trying to beg enough money for a bite to eat. 'Got any money mate?' is the usual request, but nowadays the beggars seem to be more aggressive. Some of them, as soon as they see someone approach, get in their face, invade their space and cause them to change direction. Then there are the piss heads, who look for a fight with anyone. 'What the fuck are you looking at?' and the ones that just want to rob you to fund their drug habit. Should you need a Policeman, there is none to be seen, just the CCTV cameras watching your every move, just in case you decide to piss in a shop doorway, or your dog fouls the pavement.

After purchasing their portions of fish cake, chips and mushy peas, Andy and Sandra head for the sanctuary of the River Gardens, a well-known local landmark, which provides a peaceful spot away from the hustle and bustle of the City Centre. They could sit in relative safety there. If it were daytime, they'd be watching the swans and ducks vying for the food being thrown into the water of the River Derwent by young children and the sound of water cascading over the weir would be drowned out by the hub bub of conversation. However, at night there was little to see, just the odd duck heading off to find a place to rest for the night.

Andy had been diagnosed with Multiple Sclerosis ten years previously. A few weeks after his diagnosis, his wife decided she did not love him anymore and left him for someone else, leaving Andy to bring up their only child alone. Then, a few years later, he met his current girlfriend, Sandra. Her arrival on the scene lead to Andy's son, Simon, also known as Ash, to leave home, aged just seventeen. Sandra and Ash clashed from the moment she moved into the house. Ash thought Sandra was a scrounger and that she was only interested in his father for the financial support he could supply.

Andy had now been with Sandra for two years. She was an alcoholic, although she would never admit it. She moved in with Andy so that he could provide her with a roof over her head. When they first met each other, she was in the process of being evicted from her flat for rent arrears. After moving in with Andy she soon worked out that he was also good for free bottles of booze when her social money had run out. All she had to do was get physically and verbally abusive and he would cave in and give her the cash. Andy knew he was in an abusive relationship but he needed the companionship, so it was a case of 'put up or shut up.' This evening, Andy would find out how she really felt about him.

Sandra wheeled Andy towards the top of the wide stone steps that lead down to the river's edge and applied the brakes. There were just eight steps down to the river. Andy stared at the reflection of the City lights on the water, lost in thought.

'The waters high, it must be all that rain we've been having,' he said. 'I love it here, my old man always used to bring me here when I was a kid, we would fish in the river and sometimes he even let us have a swim if the current wasn't too strong. It's changed a lot over the years. There used to be a big pond here, planted with huge lilies and two large bronze turtle sculptures overlooking it. I wonder where they ended up…at some big nob's house no doubt, or maybe some fucker cashed them in for scrap. These chips are nice, aren't they love? Are you listening to me Sandra?'

Suddenly a hand rested on his shoulder, but it wasn't Sandra's. Andy tried to turn his head to see who was behind him but his condition restricted him, all he managed to see, from the corner of one eye, was the large figure of a man silhouetted by the lamplight.

'Who are you, where's Sandra, what's going on?'

'Fuck me, Andy, you can rabbit on a bit, I think you're losing your fucking marbles mate.'

'Where's Sandra?' Andy asked again, sounding increasingly worried.

'She sold you out Andy. She sold you for a bottle of fucking vodka, that's all your worth mate.'

The man standing behind him was Terry Gamble, otherwise known as 'Peanut', a name he had been labelled with as a child. Terry was the youngest brother of the deceased Tommy Gamble, known as 'AK', who was the former leader of 'Government' an infamous Derby criminal gang. Peanut was a scary character. He stood six foot, four inches tall and had a large burn scar which covered the whole of the right side of his face and his right hand. That hand rested on Andy's shoulder, it had two fingers missing.

'I need some information, Andy. I hope you're going to deliver.'

'What do you want?'

'I need to know where your son Ash is, he seems to have disappeared off the planet.'

'I've got news for you, so would I. Not seen him for ages,' Andy said, unconvincingly.

'Andy, Andy, Andy… don't fucking lie to me. You were seen with him yesterday. I'll ask you again. Where's Ash?'

'I know who you are, you're AK's brother, Peanut. The word on the street is you have a new nickname now, 'Mister Burns,' that's what you get for playing with fireworks.' Andy laughed nervously and carried on eating what was left of his chips.

Peanut started to laugh.

'We have a fucking comedian Josh.'

Josh, who was standing nearby, was Peanut's right-hand man and fellow gang member. Josh was equally just as crazy as Peanut. He was keeping a look out, making sure they were not disturbed.

Andy knew something bad was about to happen to him, regardless of what answer he gave. So, he threw the towel in, what will be, will be, he thought.

'Listen, whatever you're going to do, just do it, because I'll never tell you where he is, so fuck you and fuck your boyfriend.'

'Now that's a shame, a real shame.'

Peanut placed his mutilated hand tightly over Andy's mouth to stop him from shouting out. Andy felt a cold blade pierce his skin, just under his right ear.

'I asked you nicely, now tell me where the little cunt is before I drag this blade across your scrawny neck.' Peanut released his hand for a second to let Andy speak.

'Fuck you, Mister Burns!!!' were Andy's last words, just before the six-inch blade was dragged violently across his neck.

As Andy began to choke on his own blood, he bit into one of the remaining three fingers of his killer's hand. Peanut struggled to restrain him, although it wasn't long before Andy started to give up the fight. Blood oozed rapidly from the open gash across his neck and after a few minutes Andy's breathing stopped.

Peanut looked around to see if anyone else had witnessed him kill Andy. That was a complication he could do without.

'Give me the masking tape Josh, for fuck's sake, we need to get out of here.'

Peanut and Josh taped Andy's arms firmly to the arms of the wheelchair, then after a short run up, Peanut pushed the back of the chair that hard it cleared the steps and plunged into the cold water. It had been premeditated. He had planned to kill Andy that night regardless. Peanut wanted revenge for what had happened to him and Josh and his older brother, Tommy, but most of all he wanted the missing money. With their hoods pulled firmly up they turned away and walked along the dark paths beside the river, avoiding the many CCTV cameras. Sandra's battered body was discovered the following morning, half a mile downstream from Andy's body. Her handbag was found at the top of the steps beside the river, it contained the knife that had killed Andy.

Chapter 2

Two Months Earlier

I sat on my patio gazing at the small boats bobbing around in the distance on the warm waters of the Mediterranean Sea. Everything seemed too perfect. What had happened two years ago, back in Derby, was fading to just a bad memory for me. We have been living in Marbella, Spain, for nearly two years now. My partner, Chrissie, has a business here, which is booming, and she is even talking about opening a second boutique. While Chrissie is at work, my job is to look after our seventeen-month old son, Matthew, and our pet dog Felix. I had managed to get a few hours of door work at a local bar, mainly on Friday and Saturday nights, we didn't need the money but I needed to escape the confines of the villa from time to time.

What a lifestyle. They call this place the Costa del Crime. Don't ask me why I ended up here, it just seemed to be the right place to go. I must have watched too many British crime films when I was growing up, I suppose. If you want to disappear - then go to Marbella, that's what they said. That's probably why some criminals still come here. After all, I was supposed to be dead. The plan was, if I kept my head down and stayed out of trouble, things would be fine. With Chrissie bringing home the bacon I had no reason to make a noise. On the other hand, if something happened and I got into a spot of bother, then there would always be the certain sort of people around here to help a fellow Brit, for a price of course.

At one time it was common knowledge that this place was where most British crooks ended up. Many still operate here, making money from everything from bent time-share deals, to drugs smuggled in from North Africa. Nowadays it is not just the Brits who choose to make their home here. Many of the British criminals moved on a few years ago. Marbella has now become the base for a new breed of criminals. The Russians, with their AK47's, have a strong grip around here, along with the Albanians, the Irish and the remaining British, all trying to get a share of the pie. All of them using this holiday paradise as a base to organise the traffic of narcotics. Marbella is an entry point for a lot of the drugs coming into Europe because of its proximity to Africa and the reason why a lot of these groups have established their centre of operations here.

But it is not just Marbella, there are hundreds of organised crime groups based in Spain, from Madrid and Barcelona, to the neighbouring province of Cadiz and the coastal provinces of Valencia and Alicante. All offering the bosses of organised crime gangs the sort of anonymity they are seeking. They can live in large mansions and go unnoticed. These people also want to be able to enjoy the proceeds of their ill-gotten gains and they can do so in the Costa del Sol, where they can spend large amounts of money without drawing attention to themselves.

That was the last thing I wanted to get involved in. I had had my share of drugs, and look where I ended up, on the run, a nowhere man. Fuck that for a game of soldiers, I promised Chrissie that those days were gone, and a promise is a promise. Once bitten, twice shy, is what I say. Chrissie's threat was another reason for keeping me in check. She said if I ever went down that road again, she would take our son and go, and I believed her.

Chrissie hated me doing the door work, she worried I might be recognised, or slip into my old ways, what a joke. She never really knew me and what I was capable of. All she knew is what she read in the papers after the Derby incident and the snippets I fed her about my army career. I was always scared that if she knew the real me, she would run a fucking mile and who could blame her. She wanted me to keep a low profile and if she had her way, she would never let me out of the villa. Even though this was like living in paradise, you can have too much of a good thing. I needed to keep myself sane and keep my ear to the ground. If I were posing as Mister Big and putting myself about, I would understand her concerns but that is not me. Sure, I can look after myself if I need to, but all I was to everyone I met here was Matt the door man. I even acted a bit thick and anti-social so that people would avoid me, I do not want friends. I have had my fill of trusting people. There was also the matter that most of the bars were full of girls, but Chrissie had nothing to worry about on that score. I had already had my fill of women too, and anyway why would I want to fuck up what I already had. I was the luckiest man alive. Chrissie had been a model, she was funny, intelligent, beautiful and an amazing mother to our son, Matthew. We were together forever, we had both been through so much to get where we are now, so there was no way I would mess that up…or so I thought.

To almost everybody back in the UK, I was a dead man. Mickey was long gone and forgotten. Very few people knew that I was still alive and some of those are people that I would trust with my life. As for the others, I am sure I will never bump into them again, after all they had their own reasons for disappearing. I had taken the identity of my dead brother, Matt, and started a new life here in Spain. I would have to be very unlucky for someone to recognise me out here and as I was spending most of my time at the villa, I was making it even harder for them.

It was seven in the evening and we had just sat down to eat our evening meal next to the pool, it was a warm, humid evening, a far cry from those cold nights in the UK. We lived in a traditional Spanish villa, air conditioned, four bedrooms, a swimming pool, complete with patio and a secluded garden area. An idyllic property to the east of Marbella, just two kilometres away from a golf course and close to a soft sandy beach.

'You'll never guess what Mickey?' Chrissie said.

'What?' I replied. Chrissie always said that. 'You'll never guess what Mickey?' as if I'm a mind reader or something.

'I met somebody in the boutique today.'

'And?' I said, pretending to be interested, whilst I was in fact trying to listen to the football match commentary on the TV. It was a champions league match; Manchester City v Athletico Madrid.

Suddenly, she got up and turned the TV off. She knew how to grab my attention.

'Sorry, was you watching that?' she said. I gave her a sarcastic smile.

'No, you're ok. What were you saying?' I asked, to avoid an argument.

According to Chrissie, meal times were when the family came together to talk about what had happened that day, it was traditional in her family. Born to an Italian mother and

English father, she was bought up believing that meal times were special.

'I said I had a visitor today, her name was Mandy, she was really nice. Well, we got chatting and she said she was here on holiday and looking at properties for her and her partner. They are thinking of moving out here next year. She wanted some advice on setting up a business in Spain, so I closed the boutique up and we went for a coffee.'

'What have I told you Chrissie, never get too friendly with people until you get to know them properly.'

'Relax Mickey, we can't carry on like that forever. I work in a boutique so I meet people all the time and I am a good judge of character. This Mandy is a lovely woman, you'd like her, and she's got a wicked sense of humour.'

I couldn't blame Chrissie for wanting to make friends, we'd tried not to make too many of them since arriving in Spain. However, if you make yourself too reclusive, people start to talk and talk leads to gossip, which leads to rumours, and before you know it, there is a knock at the door.

'Anyway, it turns out that she used to run a pet shop in the UK and she is looking at doing the same out here' Chrissie said.

'A pet shop, eh.' I tried to sound interested whilst attempting to grab the remote, but she beat me to it.

'Are you listening to me Mickey?'

'Yes of course I am, so what did you say to her?'

'I said go for it, to be honest, I haven't seen any pet shops near here, have you?'

'You called me Mickey!'

'Did I?'

'Yes! We had an agreement to never call me Mickey, it's important Chrissie.'

'Ok, don't get all serious on me Mickey, we're in our own home.'

'I don't care; we agreed never to call me Mickey again. If they found out Mickey was still alive, it would open up a whole world of trouble.'

'If who found out? We live in Spain remember.'

'It doesn't matter where we live Chrissie.'

'I'm still waiting for you to tell me what happened that night, I only know what was printed in the papers and you have never told me about how your brother died. Maybe if you did, I would understand the reason for the nightmares you are having and what it is you are running away from'.

Her last sentence made me see red. I stood up and raised my voice.

'Running! I'm not running away from anyone. I never have and never will. We are here in Spain because we wanted to be here, it's what we wanted, way before all that happened. We planned it remember. I changed my name to protect you and our kid. Trust me, we definitely don't want me to be Mickey again.'

The silence hung between us for a few minutes, this was the first time I had raised my voice to Chrissie since the time when she lived in her flat in London. She got up to check on Matthew, I followed her into his room, he was sound asleep.

'Isn't he beautiful?' she said.

'Yes, he is' I replied as I slipped my arms around her neck.

'Sorry Chrissie, I love this life, I don't want anything to spoil it.'

'Me too. We're lucky, aren't we?' We started to kiss.

'There's only one thing missing.'

With that, she took a step back looking puzzled, wondering what I was going to say next.

'Any chance of having the football back on now?'

'No!'

We made our way back to the patio.

'Anyway, I've invited her around tomorrow night for a bite to eat and a chat. I told her I would give her all the knowledge I could about starting a business in Spain because as you know, it can be a minefield if you don't know what you're doing. I don't mind helping her.'

'What about me? I don't want to sit around listening to all that rubbish.'

'Come on don't be like that, as I said, she's a really nice person, you'll get on with her like a house on fire.'

'I've just remembered I'm working tomorrow night. She'll be gone before I get home.'

'So, does that mean she can come around then?'

'Yes, I suppose she can.'

Having got me to agree, she turned the TV back on, so that I could watch the last twenty minutes of the match.

The next day, after looking after Matthew all day, I put him to bed early. I usually let him stay up until his mum came home, but today was different. Today Chrissie was bringing her mystery friend home. I had been tasked to prepare dinner before my escape to work, which was easy, it was just a case of putting the barbie on and preparing the meat and side salad. I heard Chrissie's car pull up on the driveway. I checked on Matthew before joining them on the patio.

'Matt, this is Mandy.' Chrissie said by way of introduction.

'Nice to meet you Matt.'

My jaw dropped to the floor, I could not believe my eyes, the person standing in my house was Lisa, AK's ex-girlfriend. The last time I saw her was when she stood over her boyfriend's dead body, just after he had had the top of his head blown off by his brother Colin, now her lover. I thought I was dead that day, until they intervened in such a dramatic way to save my life. They double crossed AK, took what money they could find then set the house ablaze and fled.

'Is he always like that?' Mandy asked, noticing my slight hesitation.

'Nice to meet you Mandy, what would you like to drink?' I replied, recovering my composure quickly.

I tried to play it cool, as if I was meeting her for the first time, I could hardly say, 'Lisa what the fuck are you doing here?' I didn't want Chrissie to know who this woman was. Chrissie knew nothing about the day at AK's. My sweet, naive Chrissie said I would get on with Mandy like a house on fire, how fucking ironic is that?

'Chrissie tells me you're interested in pets. I used to know somebody who ran a pet crematorium business.' I said.

I should have known who Chrissie's new friend was, the cryptic clues were there. The small talk went on for a while, then the sound of Matthew crying carried out to the patio. Chrissie stood up and went off to attend to him.

'Alright Lisa why are you here, more to the point, who told you I was here?'

'You owe me Mickey.'

'Like hell I do. Where's Colin?'

'Colin's not here, it's just me. I'm on my own.'

'Who told you I was here?'

'Ash.'

'I don't believe you. Ash would never tell you where I was.'

'He would if he is in hiding, fearing for his life.'

Just then Chrissie came back out onto the patio.

'Talking in his sleep again, just like his dad. Where were we?'

There was an awkward silence before Chrissie spoke again.

'So, what would you like to eat, Mandy?'

'I'll tell you what Chrissie, I'm not feeling that well, I think it's something I ate earlier today, bloody Spanish food.'

'Oh, sorry to hear that, another time perhaps?'

'Can you order me a taxi.'

'No need, he's just off to work aren't you Matt, he can drop you off at your hotel. Is that ok with you babe?'

'Sure, if you want.' I had no choice but to agree, even though her new friend was the last person I wanted to give a lift to.

Chrissie and Lisa said their goodbyes, then she climbed into my car and we left. We said nothing to each other for the first part of the journey back to her hotel.

'Nice little set up you've got there, Mickey. You've done alright for yourself, haven't you?' she said, breaking the silence.

I pulled off the road into a layby. I knew I would not be able to concentrate on the road until I found out why she had tracked me down.

'So, what's this all about Lisa, one minute I feel on top of the world, then you appear, and my world all comes crashing down.'

'Mickey I'm not here to spoil your paradise. I'm not that kind of person.'

With that comment she placed her hand on my leg. She slowly moved her hand up towards my crotch.

'What are you doing?'

'I have an empty room back in the hotel' she replied, smiling.

I lifted her hand away from my leg and placed it back in her lap.

'You're ok, I'll give that one a miss thanks.' I said.

She then pulled a newspaper out of her bag and handed it to me. A quick glance told me it was an English newspaper.

'Here, you need to read this, it might interest you.' she said looking directly at me.

The front cover headline reads: 'EX GANG MEMBERS RELEASED - CHARGES DROPPED.' I sat there and read the report, I could not believe what I was reading.

'What, they've let them go?' I was shocked by what the paper had printed.

Peanut and his side kick, Josh, had spent twenty months on remand charged with murder, now all charges had been dropped.

'Insufficient fucking evidence? They must be having a laugh. I thought they were going down for a long time.' I handed the paper back to Lisa. 'So, what's that got to do with me?' I asked, pretending I had no interest in the report.

'His brother is dead, Mickey, Ash is alive. Where did the weed go and the money? Peanut will not rest until he finds out. You need to get rid of him Mickey, before he gets to Ash. What if Ash tells him you are alive and where you are, then what? Your little version of paradise could be over.'

'He won't do that, and anyway, why don't you shut him up? I seem to remember your boyfriend Colin is quite handy with a gun. Why should all this bother you Lisa, you don't live in Derby anymore do you?'

'He's Colin's brother as well you know. He told Colin he would not rest until he had his revenge. Ash is in hiding but I am sure it won't take Peanut long to track him down.'

'But it was Colin who fucking killed him, not me or Ash.'

'Yes, to save your life, but Peanut doesn't know that. Think about it Mickey, if you sort this then it's the perfect murder, everybody thinks you're dead, remember.'

'I'll sort it.' I answered, knowing I would never feel safe while Peanut was alive.

'When?'

'I'll sort it,' I replied angrily.

I took a few deep breaths to calm myself down then pulled out of the layby and headed towards Lisa's hotel. I had the feeling there was more to Lisa's appearance in Spain than Peanut's release.

'That's not the only reason you're here is it Lisa, surely you didn't come out here just to tell me that, you could have sent me a post card.'

'Can we go somewhere quiet; I have a proposition for you.'

'If it's anything to do with what happened a few minutes ago, I told you, I'm unavailable.'

'No, it's nothing like that, you need to find somewhere quiet so that we can talk.'

I had no interest in anything else she had to say, she had said enough already. I was more concerned about what I had just found out. However, she had come all this way, so the least I could do is hear her out. I took her to where I worked part-time, 'Pep's Bar.' A quiet place in the daytime, mainly serving food to holiday makers staying in the self-catering apartments nearby. In the evening, the place came alive with live bands playing most nights between the months of April and September. I was not due to start work for another half hour, I felt safe there, amongst friends.

We sat inside, in a quiet spot. Don't ask me why, but I had a vision of someone driving by and taking a pot shot at me, maybe I was being a bit paranoid, it pays to be cautious sometimes, it saved my life many times in Afghanistan. While she sat at the table I went to the bar and ordered two beers from Pep, the manager.

'Sure, Matt, I'll bring them over to you.'

I went back to the table and sat down. Even though I would never go anywhere near Lisa, she was an attractive woman and she knew it.

'Nice place Mickey, you work here you say?'

She started to look around as though she was looking for somebody, maybe she was being cautious, like me, or just being nosey.

'I'd rather you called me Matt in here.'

'Oh, sorry, I get it Matt. You don't have to call me Mandy by the way.'

I had no interest in any small talk, I wanted to know the real reason for her visit.

'Just tell me what you have to say Lisa.'

'Ok, I'll keep this short. I need a favour Matt.'

'What sort of favour?'

'You've been here for a while now. I am sure you've built up a few contacts. I was wondering if you could put me in touch with the right people?'

I leant back in my chair as Pep approached us and placed two beers on the table. He stood looking at Lisa for a short time before returning to the bar. I waited for him to walk away out of earshot before I replied.

'What do you mean the right people?'

'Do I have to spell it out? I'm here doing a little business on behalf of a friend of mine.'

'You mean Colin?'

She laughed.

'Forget it Lisa, that's not going to happen.'

'But you haven't heard me out yet, I have a lot of money to put on the table. You do this for me and you'll be upgrading from that shack you're living in.'

'For your information, I'm quite happy with my villa. What is it you're after anyway?' I asked, trying to figure out what she wanted from me.

'Cocaine, we used to have a contact over here, but it dried up when AK sadly passed away.' she said, smiling. 'Listen, like I said, I'm willing to spend a lot of money Matt, and there's a big slice of the cake for you, if you can help us out.'

'Why can't you get it in the UK, is nobody selling it anymore?'

'Not in the quantity we can get it over here or the price.'

'Who the fuck do you think I am, some sort of drug lord? I'm just Matt the doorman that's all. Have you any idea what you are getting into, you are talking about the Russians or Albanian's aren't you? From what I have heard these guys don't play fair, so go home, I'm not introducing you to anybody, even if I knew how to. I'm sorry.'

'That is a pity, a real pity, you owe me, Mickey. I thought with you working in this bar you would have some contacts,' she said loudly.

'And why would you think that? Like I said, I am not interested and I don't owe you anything. I'll sort the Derby problem out for you and that's it.'

Lisa stood up and finished her beer as quickly as you would if last orders had just been called.

'I'll give you six weeks Mickey and then you'll be in touch, begging us to let you get involved, you'll see. Your money won't last forever.'

'Chrissie is doing just fine, we don't need any money, especially anymore drug money.'

Lisa looked disappointed by my reply.

'Colin always gets what he wants Mickey, you'll see. I'll make my own back to the hotel.'

She walked out of the bar without looking back, but I knew it wouldn't be the last time I would hear from her. I got up from the table and made my way to the bar and ordered another drink from Pep.

'Aren't you supposed to be working for me tonight?' he asked as he served me the beer.

'Yes, I'm a bit early.'

'Who was that?'

'Just an old friend, I bumped into her earlier today. Why do you ask?'

'She called you Mickey?'

'Oh, it was a name I used at the time, you know how it is Pep and before you say anything I'm not playing away, she isn't my type.'

'Good, keep it that way or I'll tell Chrissie.'

'I believe you Pep.'

'Chrissie's a nice girl, you've got a good one there, Mickey.'

Pep came around from the bar and stood beside me. He leaned in close and whispered.

'But if there's any chance of you fixing me up with this Lisa. I'm all ears.'

'Piss off Pep, you dirty old man. I wouldn't bother, she'd suck you in and spit you out.'

'My type of girl then.' he chuckled.

It was a busy night, busier than usual but around one in the morning things started to die down. The only people left in the bar were two young couples and a guy sitting on his own. It was not usual to see a guy sat on his own in a bar like Pep's, unless he was waiting for his mate or girlfriend. There was something about him, he sat with his back to the wall and his eyes were darting all over the place. I don't know why it is, but most ex-military can spot ex-military a mile off. I doubted he had been here in Spain long, if his pasty skin colour was anything to go by. We made eye contact. He nodded his head, as though he knew me. He then stood up, picked up his drink and then sat down at the bar, a few bar stools away. After a short pause, he ordered another drink.

'Another one of these, please, fella.'

That one word was a dead give-away. Personally, I hated the word 'fella.' He was either in the military or a veteran.

'I know you,' he said.

I turned my head slowly to meet his gaze, wondering if this was going to be a day for meeting old ghosts.

'Really, I don't know you.'

'Mickey isn't it, Mickey Saunders, I remember you.'

'Nah mate, you've got the wrong bloke, my name is Matt.'

'I never forget a face Mickey.'

I stood up to confront him. I stared into his eyes. This was fucking bizarre, all these things happening in one day, was I dreaming all this? I was expecting Chrissie to wake me up any minute.

'What was it they used to call you, M&M, mental Mick? I joined on your last tour of Afghanistan. You were a legend, Mickey, I heard what happened to you and your section, respect buddy, they still spoke about you and your brother way after you left.'

'I think you've been playing too much 'Call of Duty', pal.' I replied.

This guy, who I didn't know, had just made it all come flooding back. I was lying on my back with a mouth full of dust, the sound of gunfire and panic all around. 'Get up! Come on Mickey… we need to get the fuck out of here.' The Taliban were everywhere. My brother lay dead next to me and my best mate was badly injured, I didn't want to get up, I couldn't get up. I just laid there staring at the clear night sky. The sound of the gunfire faded, silence, and then the sound of the Chinook that took us to safety. That was it, my army career that I loved, was over. I hadn't visited that scene for a while, this was my first flash back since I left the UK.

'Listen, FELLA! I don't know who the fuck you are, and who the hell you're talking about, ok.'

We were now full on face to face. He placed his hand on my chest to stop me from getting closer.

'Woah, woah, I haven't come here for trouble, no dramas mate. What did you say your name was, Matt was it? You must be his double.'

'Problem Matt?' Pep asked, from his position behind the bar.

'No, everything's cool Pep, this guy's about to leave.'

'We're about to close my friend, so if you can finish your drink.' Pep urged him.

With that, he stood up, lit a cigarette, smiled at me and left.

'What was all that about? He was convinced he knew you.'

'I know, he wouldn't give up would he, it must be this place Pep, it attracts the weirdos.'

I passed Pep my glass.

'Put us another whiskey in there, will you.'

Pep would always let me have free drinks at the end of the night, providing that I stuck around while he shut up the bar and put the takings in his little hideaway, a bit of security for a few free drinks, that was the deal. I always made the most of it. Pep knew nothing about me, what I liked about him was he never asked about my past and how I ended up in Spain. There had been a few incidents since I started working for him, usually involving pissed up Brits who thought they could take on the world. Most of the time I was able to calm the situation down, but sometimes it needed a little bit more than that, he knew I was more than capable of looking after myself and felt safe in my presence. Pep was not the owner of the bar, he was just the manager. From what I understood, the bar owners were Albanians…say no more. Whether they belonged to the local Albanian mafia, who knows, probably. You never ask that sort of question and quite frankly I didn't want to know. I had made that very clear to Pep one evening.

'If you want me to, I can put in a good word for you, there's always a place for someone like you.' He said, after observing my handy work when a violent brawl started in the bar, which I quickly sorted out.

'You're ok Pep.' It was obvious Pep had 'connections.'

I sat at the bar on my own for a while. I had to figure out what the fuck was going on, what a day. Then my thoughts turned to Ash. So, the mighty 'Peanut' is running things in Derby now, which means it would only be a matter of time before he got to Ash and then to the rest, such as Katie, Debbie and Daz. I had no choice, I needed to get back to the UK and take care of things.

'Pep can you do me a favour? I need to get back to the UK for a few days, there's some business I need to sort out.'

I knew Pep would be able to help because I had overheard him making travel arrangements for other people in the past.

'Leave it with me Mickey. I'll let you know tomorrow.' With Pep you never got a straight answer. He finished his sentence with, 'it will cost you.' Everything had a price.

My taxi arrived and it was time to head home. I would pick my car up in the morning. When I arrived back at the villa, Chrissie was still up and she opened the door when she heard the taxi pull up. I kissed her at the door.

'You waited up?'

'Yes, I couldn't sleep. Did you get her back to the hotel ok?'

'Who?' I asked, my mind still on the journey ahead of me.

'Mandy. Surely you've not forgotten her already.'

'Oh yes, she's safely back at her hotel. It's been a busy night babe, I'm shattered.'

'I'll have to check in on her tomorrow to see if she's alright, before I go to work. Do you want a coffee?'

'Why not, go on then.'

While she made the coffee, I sat and debated whether to tell her I needed to be away for a few days, I knew she would not be happy. That was an understatement, she would do her nut and do everything she could to stop me. I had no reason to be away from her and Matthew, she would smell a rat straight away. When she arrived back with the coffee, we made our way out to the patio and lay on the sun loungers, there was a cool breeze blowing. Looking out over the Mediterranean, we could see an electrical storm in the distance, an amazing scene.

'I wonder if it's coming our way?' Chrissie asked.

'Maybe,' I answered.

'Ok, out with it, what's bugging you?'

'There is nothing bugging me,' I replied.

I decided I would not tell her my plans, not until I had heard from Pep the following day. I reached over and grabbed her hand. I felt guilty about not telling her.

'There's nothing wrong Chrissie. I'm just so happy here.'

Chrissie smiled. She didn't ask me again that night. Maybe the electrical storm was a warning to me of what was to come!

Chapter 3

I awoke the next morning around nine o'clock, unusually late for me. I shot out of bed to see if Matthew was ok but his cot was empty. I panicked, until I read the note on the kitchen table.

'Gone to work, took Matthew with me. You looked like you needed a lay in, meet me for lunch, love you xxx.'

I had a shower and got ready for my lunch date with Chrissie. I checked my phone for the time and saw that there was a text from Pep.

Good news on trip to UK, can you go Monday morning 9am?

That was quick, I thought. I texted back.

Yes, no worries, see you later.

Today was Saturday. I knew I would have to tell Chrissie tonight about my plans. I wasn't looking forward to it, she was going to kick off, I was certain of it. We met at the usual place, just up from the boutique. It was always a cappuccino and cake. Chrissie loved her cake. It amazed me, she could eat cake until it was coming out of her ears, but she never, ever, put any weight on.

'So, did you manage to see Mandy?' I asked.

'No, she wasn't in her hotel. I sent her a text and told her I would see her on Monday. What are you up to for the rest of the day?'

'Not much. I need to pop in and see Pep that's all. Then I am all yours,' I said, giving her a peck on the cheek.

'Great we can go down to the beach later. What are you seeing Pep about?'

'He wants me to work a few extra days.'

'Ok, ask him when he's coming around for tea. I'd love to see him again.'

'I will.' I looked at my watch. 'Right, I'll be off, see you later and you too, trouble,' I said, ruffling my son's hair.

I walked the short distance to Pep's Bar. In the distance, not far from the hotel Lisa was staying at, there was a car, inside was the guy I met the night before. He was sitting in the car with another guy, who looked like one of the locals. I thought nothing of it and walked into the bar. If he had been on his own, I would have approached the car and tapped on the window to apologise. I was well out of order the way I spoke to him the previous night. The guy was just trying to be friendly, everything he said made sense. He must have been in my unit. I suppose it was inevitable that I would eventually bump into someone from my past.

The bar was open when I arrived, it was relatively quiet, just a few customers being served lunch. I walked up to the bar where Pep stood, keeping a watchful eye over his clientele.

'Good morning Matt, beer?' he asked.

'Better make it a coke, Pep.'

'So, you're ok for Monday?'

'Yes, I've just got to tell Chrissie.'

'It's going to cost you five thousand euro I'm afraid.'

'How much!'

'That is the going rate Matt, but it's a guaranteed passage. These guys were smuggling people into the UK way before the illegals started surging in. Have you got the five thousand? If you haven't, I can lend it to you, I don't mind, I know you're good for it.'

'It's ok Pep, I have the money and thanks, I owe you.'

'No problem good friend, you be careful, whatever you're going back for.'

Pep handed me a piece of paper with the details of where to be and what time my pickup was.

'Like I said, I'll be back in a few days, Friday, hopefully. You'll manage without me, won't you?'

'Back Friday, how are you getting back?'

'Getting out of the UK is a lot easier than getting in, don't worry I have that sorted.'

He had no idea that I was using my dead brother's identity. It was easy getting out of the UK because there were hardly ever any checks, just a quick glance at your passport. Getting in was a different story.

I drove my car back to the villa, got changed and went for a run, to clear my head. I was not looking forward to telling Chrissie about my plans for Monday. Arriving home later, I decided to tell Chrissie my intentions. As I predicted, she went crazy.

'Why Mickey, why now?'

I didn't berate her for calling me Mickey. The 'call me Matt' game had failed miserably. I gave up with that one.

'I just need to sort a few things out.'

'Sorry, that's not good enough, what things?'

'Things.'

She then threw the newspaper, that she had found in the car, down on the table; she was one step ahead of me.

'It's not something to do with this by any chance?'

She had obviously read the article.

'There are no prizes for guessing what that's all about. It even mentions your name.'

She had caught me off guard. I didn't say anything for a few seconds. Chrissie stood there, with her hands on her hips, waiting for a response.

'Well fucking go then you idiot, you're supposed to be dead, remember? What's up, do you want to die for real this time? There's only one reason you want to go back to Derby and that's for revenge.'

Chrissie began to cry as she turned and walked away. I followed her to the bedroom and I stood in the doorway as she began to pack a suitcase.

'What are you doing?'

'I told you Mickey. I've always said that if you ever went down that road again then that would be it, you wouldn't see me again…and I meant it.'

'You don't understand, I haven't got a choice.'

'Wrong, you have got a fucking choice. It's either that life, or me and your son…and it's plainly obvious to me which one is more important to you.'

'Please don't go Chrissie.'

'You don't get it do you? Stupid man, get out my way please.'

'Where are you going to go?'

'I'm going to stay in the flat above the boutique. I can't stay here tonight.'

'Chrissie there's things I can't explain. I just know that if I don't go back and sort this, then they'll come looking.'

'Thing's you can't explain, that's a new one, I've never heard that one before, have I Mickey? Like what? Go on, tell me.'

I wanted to tell her the whole story but I was scared she would leave anyway if she found out about the real me. I grabbed her with both hands, prepared to plead with her.

'Let go of me,' she said in a cold, detached voice.

I let her go, at least she wasn't leaving me for good, yet. Maybe a night apart would give her time to think. She put her case in the car, strapped baby Matthew in the back, put Felix on the seat beside him and drove off. Chrissie was a stubborn woman, when she said something, she meant it. There were no goodbyes. As much as I wanted to, I wouldn't be able to stop her, she was probably better off without me anyway.

I was awoken early the next morning by the persistent ringing of the doorbell, it rang and rang. I knew it wasn't Chrissie because she had a key. I jumped out of bed and peered through the blinds. Two Spanish Police officers stood at the door. Shit, I instantly thought they must be after me, they had finally caught up with me. The thought crossed my mind that Chrissie had told them who I was, but I knew deep down she would not do that. There were all sorts of alarm bells going off in my head. I hid in the bedroom until they drove away, what the hell was that all about?

Sitting down on the bed, I grabbed my phone, intending to call Chrissie, but when I looked at my phone, I saw four missed calls from Pep. Strange, I thought, what does he want? It must be important, maybe something to do with the trip I was planning to make. I chose not to call him back. Whatever it was, it could wait. The appearance of Police officers at my door had got me worried.

I thought Chrissie would have returned home by now, then I realised it was Sunday morning, which meant she would be opening the boutique about now, hoping to make a few sales from those who worked all week. I decided to head to the boutique and tell Chrissie everything was ok and that I'd decided I was not going to make the trip because she was right. After lying awake most of the night, thinking things through and battling my demons, I came to my senses. That chapter of my life was over, what had I been thinking. I was staying put. If they did come over here looking for me, well, bring it on, at least it would be on my turf. But, before I could give Chrissie the good news, I needed to tell Pep the trip was off.

I left via the back gate and took an alternative route along the beach front, just in case anyone was watching the villa. I needed to know why the Police had been at our door. Twenty minutes later, I approached the bar whilst constantly checking to make sure no one was following me. Something caught my eye, there seemed to be a lot of commotion going on further down the street. The area was cordoned off from the public, who were eager to catch a glimpse of the unfolding events. At first, I thought it was some sort of terrorist incident, or a serious car crash. There were police cars and fire engines lining the street and the fire crews were sitting on the ground, looking exhausted, evidently, they'd had a busy time.

A shiver went down my spine because the boutique was down there. Chrissie and the baby are at the boutique, are they ok? I increased my pace and almost ran towards the scene, my only thought was to get to Chrissie and Matthew. Then I spotted Pep, he was walking towards me, coming from the direction of the incident. When he reached me, he opened his arms, like he was trying to prevent me from seeing something.

'Matt, come inside,' he urged, grabbing my arm.

'What is it Pep, what's happened?'

'You need to come inside,' he said, trying to force me off the street and into the bar.

I resisted his efforts to drag me into the bar.

'It's not good Matt. You do not want to go down there. It's the boutique, it's gone.'

It suddenly felt like all the blood from my body had drained away. I felt weak and light- headed. The only thing holding me up was Pep's strong grip around my shoulders.

'They've found two bodies Matt. Where are Chrissie and Matthew?' Pep asked.

I did not answer him, I could not speak. Pep's last sentence was like being punched in the stomach. I took a few deep breaths to steady myself and walked towards the cordon. Pep was behind me, still attempting to drag me back to the bar. Reaching the cordon, I was stopped by a Police officer. I could see two body bags on the ground, one large and one small. That said it all, it was a sight that would haunt me forever. I knew it was them. I could see Chrissie's arm hanging loosely from the partly zipped body bag. She was wearing the silver watch and the bangle I had bought her for her birthday. I wanted to run towards them and cuddle them both, but knew I couldn't. What good would it do? I turned away from the heartbreaking scene and walked back towards the bar. Pep stood outside, waiting for me. As I drew level with him, he tried to embrace me, but I stepped back and walked past him and kept walking without looking back. Everything was muffled, as though I was in a bubble. I could hear Pep shouting me.

'Matt, where are you going?' I ignored him.

Now I knew the reason for the Police visit and the missed calls. I walked back to our home as though in a trance, it still hadn't hit me properly yet. The only thought in my mind was to get back to the villa, maybe Chrissie was waiting for me there, it couldn't be them in those bags. This was a nightmare surely, I'll wake up any minute I thought, but it wasn't a bad dream, it was real.

Arriving back at the villa I walked around shouting their names continually. 'Chrissie! Matthew!' I walked into my son's bedroom, his cot was empty, in our bedroom, so was our bed. I sat down on the bed and tried to make sense of what had happened. I knew the Police would be back. I had a decision to make and quickly. I sat there just staring, then the nightmare began…

He's dead, there's nothing we can do. We need to get the fuck out of here Mickey.
I'm not going without him. There was hardly anything left of my brother lying there in the blood-soaked sand, just body parts. We were now under heavy fire. I grabbed what I could and got out of there.

I woke up from my flash back with a jolt. It had been a recurring nightmare at times of stress. I hurriedly packed what I could, it would only be a matter of time before the Police appeared again. Money, clothes, souvenirs, the handgun that was taped under the bed, which Chrissie never knew was there, a bottle of brandy. There was so much I wanted to take. Clues to my identity were everywhere. I wanted to take it all, but I couldn't. This had been our paradise and nobody could have any of this. There was only one thing for it. I took two bottles of BBQ fuel and emptied both bottles where I could, then made my way to the door. I took one last look at the place, the memories we shared were all going to disappear now. I flicked the lighter and lit the fuel-soaked sofa. It did not take long before the villa was ablaze.

I walked along the beach and kept walking and walking, past the sunbathers who were looking up at the trail of smoke, suddenly it was grabbing everyone's attention. The further I walked, the less interest there was in the trail of smoke. Behind me, the distant sound of the fire engine sirens reminded me of what I had done. I walked for hours without turning back, I must have covered at least ten miles. There were no more tourists around, just a few locals and fishermen.

It began to get dark, so I found myself an isolated spot on the beach and sat down. The sun was setting, a scene I usually enjoyed watching, but my mind was blank. I must have sat there for hours, my mouth felt dry, I needed a drink. I remembered that I had a full bottle of brandy in my bag and although I had never been a big drinker, I managed to drink almost all of it. I woke up sometime later, water was covering my feet, the tide was coming in.

I looked at my wrist to see the time, but my watch was gone and so was my bag, my ring and the pendant from around my neck, which held photos of Chrissie and Mathew. Now I had nothing, apart from a few wet euros in my pocket, my phone and the gun which was tucked into the waistband at the back of my trousers.

I took the phone out of my pocket to check the time and that is when I saw the text message from Chrissie. All the missed call notifications from Pep had partially hidden it. I hesitated before opening the message…would reading it push me over the edge? I decided to read it, as it was the only link left to my beautiful Chrissie.

Mickey, I'm sorry about tonight, if you want to go and sort things out then go. I understand. I can't change who you are babe. I love you just hurry back to me xxx

Seeing the text from her made me realise just how much I had lost and it hit me big time. I cried like a baby until I had no more tears to shed. The beach began to fill with tourists again, the sun was shining brightly. I had no idea what to do next. I had no choice but to call Pep.

I sat and watched the holiday makers splashing around in the sea with not a care in the world. Oh, how I wished I could be like them. It wasn't too long before Pep arrived to pick me up. I was surprised when he took me to his house. He did not ask me any questions; I think he could tell I was a broken man.

'I think you need some time on your own Matt,' he said, after making me a cup of coffee.

'My name's Mickey, Pep.'

If there was one person who deserved to know who I really was, it was Pep. He had done so much for me and Chrissie when we first arrived in Spain. He had been like an honorary grandfather to Matthew.

'You can't stay here Mickey; the Police have already been in the bar asking questions. I told them you were just a guy who helped me out at the bar from time to time, that is all. I have a good friend who has a small yacht docked in the marina, he said you could stay there for as long as you need to.'

Pep's suggestion sounded like a good idea. I needed time on my own to plan my next move. I finished my coffee and Pep drove me to my new accommodation. It was perfect, very roomy inside, equipped with everything I needed, including a TV and the cupboards were full of food. Pep sat inside with me for a while, we had a cold beer.

'Well, what do you think?'

'It's great Pep, you're a good man, I owe you.'

'You just get yourself right, it doesn't matter how long it takes. To be on the safe side, I will not come and see you or contact you for a few weeks, the Police are asking too many questions. Setting fire to the villa was not the wisest thing to do. Don't worry though, their activity will die down soon, trust me, I know how it works here. This is the Costa del crime, sorry to say it Mickey, but they've got worse things than this to worry about,' Pep said, as he walked towards the door that lead to a short flight of steps and off the boat. He reached the door, turned towards me and handed me a backpack that he had carried onto the boat.

'These may come in handy,' he said, before making his way off the boat.

I locked the door behind him and it would stay locked. Opening the backpack, I found several pairs of shorts, flip flops, some t-shirts and vest tops. I was glad that Pep was on the ball because I hadn't given a thought to any clothes, even though I only possessed what I was wearing. I took up hermit status for about five weeks. I rarely left the boat, and if I did, it was only late at night, just now and again to get fresh supplies. I had countless sleepless nights, and the only sleep I did get was plagued with nightmares. My mind was tearing me apart. I felt guilty because I was still living and breathing, and Chrissie and Matthew had died. I had felt like this before, when I had failed to bring my brother home, always wondering what I could have done differently to save him. Now it had happened again and it was my fault, it's a war within myself that I don't think will ever go away. I am so fucking tired of being alive. It is so exhausting. And it only seemed to be getting worse. What do you do when there is nothing left to do? Sun comes up, sun goes down.

Pep kept his word and I did not see him again until the sixth week, when he came with some news that I didn't expect. He told me that my son was alive and well. Matthew had survived the fire. It wasn't him in the small body bag, it was our dog, Felix. I could not control my emotions; I was both happy and sad in equal measures. I had lost everything that reminded me of Chrissie and now I'd been told that my son was alive, the little person that was part of both of us. Suddenly I didn't feel like dying anymore.

He also told me that despite the inquest they were still no nearer to finding out how the fire had started.

Chrissie's body had been flown back to the UK for burial, this had been arranged by her mother. I had never met her mother, like everyone else, she never knew I who I was. Pep told me that Chrissie's mother had also took Matthew back to the UK with her. I knew he would be loved and well looked after by her. Chrissie always told me that her mum was a great woman. She had wanted me to meet her one day, but she wanted me to clear my name first. That will never happen now. Setting fire to the villa had complicated things and going back to work at Pep's was off limits for me. I would have to find some other employment. Knowing that my son had survived, I had hoped would aid my recovery from PTSD, my army days was always there. I had learnt to control it during my time in Spain, but now it was back with a vengeance and now there was nobody lying next to me at night to tell me that I just was having a bad dream. The flash backs always occurred when I was full of rage or stressed out and I could not control them. It was a sort of release mechanism.

I stayed on the yacht for another few weeks, happy to be alone now that I had something to live for. I started to venture out more and visited a few local bars near the marina. The holiday season was drawing to a close, so therefore fewer tourists frequented the shops, bars and restaurants.

I even started to go for walks up and down the beach, always just before sunset, when there were fewer people around, so that I wouldn't be spotted. On one of those evenings, with a bottle of brandy in my beach bag for company, I had been walking for a while, my mind deep in thought, when I passed a group of Spanish youths. I was sure I recognized one of them as we passed each other. He stared back at me with a nervous smile. I walked on another fifty yards down the beach before it came to me that he was one of the fuckers who had robbed me on the beach that day. A hazy booze filled memory of being surrounded by a group of teenagers had surfaced. I decided to turn around and confront him and it wasn't long before I'd caught up with him. I tapped him on the shoulder. He turned to face me, the nervous smile still on his face.

'I know you,' I said.

He replied in Spanish. It was then that I noticed the bastard was wearing my pendant.

'That's my fucking pendant,' I said, pointing at his neck and that's my ring!' It was the ring Chrissie had given me. Suddenly his expression changed as he realized he had been caught out. His hand went swiftly to his waist and he pulled out a large knife on me. His friends started to run away. He looked nervous as he threatened me with his knife. I stood my ground and put out my hands.

'Come on then, what are you waiting for, come on.'

At that moment I did not care what happened to me. Seeing the ring and the pendant, the only things left that reminded me of my Chrissie, sent me into a rage. I had hit rock bottom.

He made a pathetic attempt to stab me, but I soon had him on the ground with his face in the sand and his arm twisted up his back...now I had the knife. I took the pendant from his neck but I struggled to pull the ring from his finger, the harder I tried, the angrier I became. In the end, I put the knife to good use and sliced through his finger. He squealed in pain. If his friends were intending to back him up, they soon changed their minds when they heard his squeals and they disappeared into the darkness. The knife was blunt but eventually the finger gave way and I had my ring back. I let him go and he staggered away, holding his butchered hand and yelling something in Spanish. I was left alone, just me and a bottle of brandy. I sat there for what seemed like ages, swigging from the bottle and staring out at the sea. I contemplated whether to just walk into the water and swim and keep on swimming, but knowing that my son was alive stopped me from doing it. I finished the bottle of brandy and walked, unsteadily, back to the yacht. The next morning when I woke up, I thought it was all just one fucked up dream. I made a promise to myself to stop drinking heavily, as it was screwing with my mind. I staggered from the bedroom to the galley kitchen and made myself a black coffee. The once pristine interior of the yacht was beginning to look like a squat, with my clothes and unwashed dishes littered around. I made a mental note to tidy it up, god knows what Pep must have thought when he saw the state it was in. It was now the middle of February; the resort was quiet and the tourists were mostly older ones. What Pep had told me about my son had given me a new lease of life. I had something to live for. He was in a safe place with his Gran. I had promised Chrissie that if anything ever happened to her, I would always be there for our son and I intended to keep that promise. I splashed my face with cold water and gave my teeth a quick brush before heading out. Cleaning the yacht would have to wait, the cupboards were bare.

Having picked up a few essentials from the local supermarket I sat in one of the many bars, watching football on the overhead TV screen. I glanced at the guy sitting to my left and saw something that immediately caught my attention; the headlines on the front of the British newspaper that he was reading.

'Excuse me, could have your paper after you've finished with it please?' I asked.

'Sure mate, I've finished with it anyway.' He said, handing me the newspaper.

The front cover headlines read 'RIVER GARDENS MURDER PROBE'. I sat there in the bar and read the whole report twice. All kinds of thoughts raced through my mind. Who did it? It could only have been one person, AK's brother, 'Peanut', no doubt aided by Josh. Lisa had told me this would happen. He is getting his revenge. I needed to get to Derby before this scum got to Ash. I felt responsible. His father's death was my fault. I should never have dragged Ash into all this mess, he was only a kid. I hurried back towards the yacht and made a call from the public telephone at the end of the jetty.

I met up with Pep the next day and explained my situation. I needed to get back to Derby as quickly as possible. He agreed with me. He said I needed to disappear for a while, as the local Police had circulated a picture of me. I was now a wanted man in Spain. There was only one problem, I was officially broke, all our money had been tied up in the business and villa, I had nothing.

'The offer still stands Mickey, I'll put up the money and give you a little extra to help you get back on your feet. You don't need to pay me back.'

'Thanks Pep, you'll get the money back, I promise.'

I got the feeling that Pep was trying to get rid of me but not in a bad way. He just did not want the Police to catch up with me. With the boutique and our villa both being burnt out, this place held only bad memories for me now.

Chapter 4

The following morning, I had a visit from Pep about my proposed trip back to the UK, it was all set to happen tomorrow, Monday. I immediately started to gather what possessions I had and started to clean up the yacht, that was when I found the pendant and ring in my bloodstained shorts, which were shoved down the side of the bed. So, it did happen, that poor kid, he did not deserve that. What I had thought was a bad dream, was real. I was starting to do crazy stuff again. I didn't need that shit, not now. I needed to be in control, not out of control. Glancing at my reflection in the mirror I realized I had let myself go, even my own mother would have trouble recognising me now. I had adopted the Robinson Crusoe look, which would no doubt come in handy in the coming days.

I left the yacht and made a few hurried purchases with the money Pep had loaned me, after all, I could hardly arrive in the UK wearing shorts, t-shirt and flip-flops. What money I had left, after my purchases, I changed into sterling. I spent a restless night, tossing and turning restlessly, before finally giving up on the idea of sleep. I quickly washed and dressed, threw a few things in the backpack and left the yacht. Following Pep's instructions, I made my way to the pickup point. I felt totally confident that I would get back to the UK without difficulty, I trusted Pep a hundred percent. I waited around at a junction about a mile away from the village, hardly any traffic passed along the road. I saw a heavy goods vehicle in the distance. As it got closer, I could see it indicating, then it drew alongside me and pulled up.

'Are you Mickey?' the driver asked.

'Yes mate.'

'Jump in my friend.'

The passenger door opened, I hesitated for a second when I saw a hand reaching out to me.

'Let me help you boss,' offered a friendly sounding voice.

The driver made his introductions, after I had been helped up into the cab.

'Mickey, my name is Sevy and the guy sitting next to you is Yakubu. He is a regular customer of SEVY TRAVEL, aren't you Yakubu?

'That's right boss', he replied, before turning to me. 'This is your first time I take it?'

'Yes.'

I could tell I was in good company and I was going to be kept entertained for the rest of the journey, but little did I know what the guy sitting next to me, Yakubu, had been through, or his reason for entering the UK in this way.

'So, have you guys brought the money?' the driver asked us both.

We both handed over five thousand euros to the driver. We drove a short distance down the road, then pulled up outside a warehouse. Sevy got down from the cab and went into the building.

'Don't worry boss, he is just paying the man and we'll be on our way,' Yakubu informed me.

We sat in silence until Sevy reappeared a few moments later with a rough looking guy. The stranger appeared to check us both out, then patted Sevy on the back and wished him a good trip. After a few hours into the journey we had all got to know each other a little more. The vehicle I was travelling in was one of three vehicles heading for the UK in convoy, it was a genuine haulage firm, one that broke the law from time to time.

'So, what is your cargo today Sevy?' Yakubu asked.

'Tomatoes, the UK loves its tomatoes, oh and you two.'

'Do you ever smuggle anything else?' I asked.

'If you mean drugs, no,' Sevy replied. I never do that, it is too risky, the punishment is too high, anything from six to twenty years depending what it is you're smuggling. I know some of my fellow drivers smuggle on a regular basis, usually it is cannabis or heroin, sometimes cocaine. It amazes me what elaborate lengths the drug smugglers will go to, to get the stuff into the UK. I read in the paper recently that the UK Border Force have found cocaine and heroin stuffed inside children's sweets, consignments of fruit, a wheelchair seat and even a portrait of the late South African leader Nelson Mandela.'

'That's crazy.' It was hard to believe the lengths people would go to, to make a fast buck.

'All I'll agree to do, is smuggle people every now and then, I only do it because I'm in debt, I've been playing a lot of money in the casino, a little bit of people smuggling won't hurt anyone, for the right price. By the way, if the customs find you, which they won't! I get fined two thousand pounds for each illegal, so the price you guys pay outweighs the fine. Everyone is a winner, so long as you guys say you smuggled onto my truck without my knowledge. Someone else put you in there.

The bloke kept us entertained nearly all the way to Calais with his jokes and stories of previous trips. The lorry began to slow down and pulled over to the side of the road.

'Right, time to jump out guys,' announced Sevy. 'It's time to hide you away, before we get to the port.'

We all jumped out at a big layby, there were no toilets to be seen, but everyone was taking a piss into the undergrowth by the side of the road. Trucks and lorries lined the road. I wondered how many of them were carrying legitimate loads.

'I've never seen so many people taking a piss at one time,' I said, looking around.

Yakubu and Sevy laughed at my comment.

'That's because this place is called the watering hole, take a closer look around you Mickey,' Sevy said.

Then it clicked, the plants that I had taken for undergrowth, were actually cannabis plants, growing wild everywhere.

'Everyone stops off and helps the grow, it's all about give and take. We call this particular strain of weed, Piss! I often grab a few buds to keep me company when I park up for the night if my crossing is not until the next morning. It gives an all new meaning to the phrase 'Taking the Piss.' Right, it's time to show you your accommodation for the next part of the journey.'

It was a very clever concealment, just behind the cab a sealed compartment at the end of the refrigeration unit. The entry and exit were behind the cab, it was a steel trap door that had to be screwed down, so once you were in there you couldn't get out unless you were let out, not a good idea for the claustrophobic. It was a tight squeeze, but once inside it was quite roomy. At least four people could fit in there, sitting down. Both Yakubu and I climbed in. Sevy popped his head in and read us the riot act.

'Yak… you know the score, you can talk all you want when we're on the move, but when we stop, not a word. If you need to take a piss, there is a bottle in the corner ok, and a torch. That panel to your left controls the refrigeration unit next door, if you look down on the floor there are a few small holes, try not to sit on them they are for ventilation...any questions?'

'Yes,' I said. 'How long will we be in here?'

'Our crossing is at five in the morning, but there could be delays, do not worry, you will be ok, Yak's done this trip loads of times. Right, have a good trip and I'll see you on the other side.'

We heard the sound of an electric screwdriver screwing down the panel, 'our door', and that was it. I was trapped in a small space with a man I knew nothing about.

'Relax, boss, everything will be fine, you'll see.'

It seemed like ages before we arrived at where I assumed was the ferry port. During the time we were on the move, stopping and starting, we got to know each other. Although I barely knew this guy, I felt like I could tell him anything. We were both locked away in this Pandora's box for a reason. I told him my story, he told me his. Yakubu's story was shocking and helped me understand why he did what he did.

Yakubu's Story

Born in Nigeria, during the eighties, he was thirteen years old when his parents decided to leave Nigeria and head for the UK to claim asylum. His mother was a nurse and his father was a teacher, their application was granted and they became British citizens within five years.

But Yakubu could never forget what had happened back in Nigeria. Born as a twin, Yakubu's brother was murdered, beaten to death on the streets of Lagos right in front of him, just because he was different. Yusuf was an effeminate boy and because of that he was persecuted, bullied, punished, and eventually murdered. So, Yakubu decided to dedicate his life to finding his brother's killers and avenge his brother's murder. He also hated the way that corruption was destroying Nigeria. His mission was to do what he could to eradicate the greedy, corrupt people who were stealing the country's wealth. Yakubu was an assassin, or, if you prefer, a sort of modern day Robin Hood.

He told me he was returning from one of his trips. The reason he wanted to slip in and out of the UK is because he did not want anyone to know he was out of the country. He travelled in this way so that he could arrive in Benin, then slip into to Nigeria unannounced, avoiding the corrupt custom officers. He flew to Benin from Spain using his British passport. So Yakubu was coming back from his mission, I was just starting mine, I asked him if he had any tips. All he said was, kill them slowly and watch them die, it makes you stronger for next time.

We both drifted off to sleep for a while. The vehicle had stopped but the engine was still running when we heard movement. At first, we thought it could be Sevy checking his lorry, then we heard voices coming from inside the refrigeration unit. I couldn't understand the language they were speaking. I assumed they were illegals trying to get to the UK, which was bad news for us. We both knew that if *they* got caught, *we* would get caught and there was nothing we could do. Then the engine stopped, we assumed we had arrived at the ferry port. We did not hear any more sounds from the refrigeration unit, maybe they had changed their minds and jumped off. Then the voices started again, this time the voices were easier to identify. I still could not understand what they were saying, but it was obvious that Yakubu could.

'They're Nigerians,' Yakubu whispered. He listened intently to what they had to say.

I could tell he was getting increasingly frustrated and angry at what he heard.

'What is it Yak? I whispered.

'They're terrorists, boss, Boko Haram.'

'What?'

'Shush, have you got a piece of paper and a pen?'

I quickly hunted through my backpack for the notebook and pen I knew were in there. I held them up to show Yakubu.

'Quickly, write this down, 23 Randal Gardens, Manchester.'

I did as my companion asked and had just finished writing when the engine started again. We were either on the move or Sevy was getting cold.

'What is happening Yak, why do you need that address?'

'That is the address of their safe house. They were talking about what they had planned. They are without doubt a terror cell.'

'We need to tell someone, Yak.'

'Who? People will ask too many questions.'

I knew he was right, we could not risk revealing how we knew about them and their plans. I thought about this problem for a while before a solution came to mind.

We arrived at Dover around six hours later and breezed through customs, along with the load of tomatoes and unwanted guests. We knew the procedure, Sevy had told us in France that he had a safe place to drop us off, about an hour's drive from the ferry port. We could not wait to get out, we had been in that box for around sixteen hours and the piss bottle was full. We felt the lorry slowing down before it came to a stop. We soon heard the screws being unscrewed and then, along with the daylight, Sevy's smiling face appeared. We were about to wipe the smile off his face. We climbed out of our hiding place behind the cab. It felt good to be able to stretch my limbs and breathe fresh air, I could tell we were back in the UK, it was pissing down with rain.

'Home sweet home gentleman, I trust you had a comfortable journey?' Sevy asked.

The place we had arrived at was an old deserted abattoir in the middle of nowhere. An ideal place for illegal activities.

'We need to tell you something Sevy,' I said.

'What?'

I asked him to open the refrigerated unit. I told him what had happened, but not to worry because I had turned the temperature unit to minus forty. Looking inside, amongst the loose tomatoes, were four frozen men, all in their mid-twenties.

'Fuck, what have you done guys?' Sevy stood there, opening and closing his mouth like a fish out of water.

'They were terrorists Sevy. Can you imagine what would have happened to us if those guys were caught?'

'No, I'm not worried about those murdering scum bags, look at my tomatoes, they're ruined.'

Yak and I looked at each other and laughed.

'Don't worry Sevy, the tomatoes will thaw out, but what are we going to do with the dead terrorists?' Yak asked.

'Looks like we've got some digging to do before we go,' replied Sevy.

A few hours later it was job done. Sevy assured us that the bodies would never be found and they were not the only bodies dumped at this place. The land was owned by the same people who owned the haulage company that had arranged our trip. No prizes for guessing who they were. We said our goodbyes to Sevy and we were on our way, in the lift provided, to the railway station. Once we arrived at the station we were on our own. We bought our tickets and boarded the same train to London.

'So, how far are you going Yak?' I asked him, as we settled ourselves down on the train.

'Only as far London, then I'll jump on the underground to Edgware.'

'Northern Line then, I used to know someone who lived in Golders Green, long story.'

'You told me, remember? Chrissie.'

'Oh yes, I did, didn't I.'

I had told Yakubu about what had happened to Chrissie, it was still painful to think about. I also told him I intended to track down her killer and dispense my own kind of justice.

'You be careful boss.'

'Call me Mickey, Yak.'

'Be careful Mickey. The Goat Killer, that's what I'll call you from now on. After the story you told me about when you were in Afghanistan, that was so funny.'

'Yes, but it wasn't funny at the time.'

He handed me his business card, which read, 'Yakubu Dimond, Chartered accountant.'

'If you're ever in trouble and you need me, just call this number,' he said.

'Chartered accountant, bloody hell. I take it you don't mean my tax return.'

'If that's what you want. Everyone has a day job.'

'I'd give you my number, but I haven't got a phone.' I had lost my phone shortly after reading the text from Chrissie, probably during one of my drunken forays.

'Don't worry, I'll find you if you need my help. I'm an expert at tracking people down.'

After our conversation I spent some time looking out of the window, watching the landscape speed by. The day was grey and dismal, a reflection of my mood. I was returning to a life I thought was over, but not by choice. The time went by quickly and we soon arrived at Victoria station and said our goodbyes.

'It's been nice knowing you, Mickey the goat killer.'

'You too Yak, sorry, but I haven't thought of a nickname for you yet.'

'I'm sure you will.'

We parted company on the station concourse and went our different ways.

Chapter 5

I made my way to the tube for the journey to St Pancras station. I had forgotten just how crowded the tube trains could be. I spent the entire journey squashed into a corner by the door. I had a few hours to kill until I caught the evening train to Derby at seven o'clock, a journey I had made many times before. I went for a short walk until I found a café, I ordered egg, chips and beans, with a mug of tea. I had not realised how hungry I was until I found myself cleaning the plate with a slice of bread. I ordered another mug of tea and sat reading through a newspaper that I found discarded on the next table, just to kill a bit more time. During my walk back to the station I was accosted several times by prostitutes, but they soon moved on when I gave them my dead pan stare. The train left on time and it was an uneventful journey, but when the train pulled into Derby station, the memories of what had happened here almost two years ago, all came flooding back. It was as though I had never left. I walked out of the station and into town. The last bus to Heanor, a small Derbyshire town, did not leave for another twenty minutes, so I took a walk to the River Gardens, I suppose I wanted to pay my respects to Ash's dad. What kind of evil bastard would do that to a defenceless old man? The newspaper report said he was a veteran, that he had served in the Royal Navy, a Falklands veteran. I had not known that. Ash had never told me much about his family.

I arrived in Heanor and walked the short distance to where Debbie and Daz lived. Debbie was an ex-girlfriend of mine and Daz was my best friend from my army days. After the incident, they both wanted a fresh start. Daz sold his narrow boat 'The Dogs Bollocks' and Debbie sold her house, and with the money they got from the sale of both they bought their dream house in the country.

Standing outside their house, there did not appear to be anyone at home or maybe they were all in bed, surely not. Debbie was never one for an early night. Well, if they were in bed, I was waking them up. It had been a long day and it was beginning to get a bit chilly. I knocked on the door but there was no answer. Shit, I thought, what if they have gone on holiday?

I opened the side gate and went around the back of the house but there were no lights showing there either. I made my way down to the shed at the bottom of the garden and luckily it was unlocked. There was just a brick securing the door shut. I went inside, the floor was covered with an old carpet. I was so tired I decided to lie down on the floor, curl up and try and get some sleep, I had slept in worse places.

Daz and Debbie arrived home around midnight. Debbie went into the kitchen to make coffee and Daz switched on the TV. Looking out of the kitchen window, Debbie could see that the shed door was slightly ajar.

'Daz, the shed door is open, I'm sure I shut it before we left, that brick's been moved.'

'What are you worried about Deb? There's nothing in there anyway.'

Debbie was the type who could never let things lie, she needed to go out there and have a look. She took her baseball bat out of the cupboard; she had used it many times before in these types of situations. She had decided to investigate.

'Where do you think you're going?' Daz asked.

'To check the shed. I shut that door. I know I did.' said Debbie.

'No, you're not.'

'Well, you go then.' Debbie replied

'I can't, I've taken my legs off now.'

It was too late, Debbie was halfway down the path. She prodded the door fully open, using the end of the bat, and peered inside. She could now see a figure lying on the floor, inside the shed.

'Daz there's someone here, call the Police,' shouted Debbie. 'Come on let's have you out, you bastard.'

Debbie stood there with the baseball bat in the strike position, ready to pounce. She had no problem using it if she had to, as her last two lovers had found out to their cost, and I was one of them.

'Put it down Debbie,' I said. 'I don't want to lose any more teeth. You took three of them last time remember.'

'Mickey, is that you?' Hearing my voice had took her by surprise.

'Where's Daz? Shouldn't he be out here defending his property?'

'Daz has taken his legs off,' said Debbie.

'He could have used this,' I replied, holding up a skateboard.

'It is you. That could only be my Mickey coming out with a comment like that!' cried Debbie, overjoyed.

She dropped the bat and threw her arms around me, hugging me tightly. My feelings for her came bubbling to the surface. It did not matter what had happened in the past, our lives had moved on. Debbie was my first love and there was still a bond between us that could never be broken.

'I've so missed you Mickey, you wouldn't believe how much. You bloody stink by the way and that beard does nothing for you. What is that smell? I suppose you'd better come in.'

I followed Debbie back up the garden and into the house. Daz was sitting in a chair near the door.

'Fine bloody hero you are, letting your missus go out there on her own,' I said, laughing.

'When have I ever been able to stop her, you know what she's like Mickey,' Daz replied. 'How are you mate?'

I hugged my old friend tightly and patted him on the back. It was good to see him looking so well.

'I'm fine Daz, just fine.'

I was soon sitting comfortably in their cosy sitting room with my hands wrapped around a hot mug of tea. It wasn't long before we began chatting about old times, all of us being careful not to mention the incident that had forced me to leave the country. It was too soon for that. I still felt guilty about what Daz had endured because of me.

For want of something to say I asked, 'where are the kids?'

'They're staying with my mum, it was our anniversary yesterday,' Debbie answered.

'You did get married then. You kept that quiet, congratulations.'

'Thanks, we've been married a year now but it only feels like yesterday,' Debbie replied.

That hurt me a little. I always thought that Debbie and I would marry one day, but it was not to be, that was another story. I was happy for them, that they had found each other.

I put on a sad face. 'So, where was my invite to the wedding, then?' I asked.

Debbie looked embarrassed. 'I'm sorry Mickey, but with what happened we thought it best that…'

I began to laugh.

'Shut up Mickey you idiot.' Debbie said, thumping me lightly on the shoulder.

I always loved winding her up. She always fell for it.

'So, what's life like out there?' Daz asked.

'Amazing, you ought to see the place. I'm so happy, and Matthew is nearly two now.'

I didn't want to burden them with any of my shit. I knew that if I told them about what had happened to Chrissie, they would feel the need to look out for me.

'You called him Matthew, after your brother, nice touch Mickey. We still go to his grave now and then, don't we Debbie? And we take him a few cans, like you did. That was before all that shit kicked off with Ash's dad. We haven't been back since it happened, I didn't fancy putting a target on my back.' Daz hesitated 'I take it you know about what happened to his dad and all that, that's why you're here isn't it? Did you hear Peanut and his sidekick are out of prison?

'Yes, I read it in the paper, I've got no doubts it was him that killed Ash's old man. You'd have thought the Police would have pulled them in by now.'

'They're probably still gathering evidence, after all they don't want to fuck up again, do they? Those two wankers have already spent nearly two years in and out of jail on remand. How would that look if they got it wrong again,' said Daz. 'Mickey I'm not being funny, but you should have stayed in Spain.'

'What are you talking about? I've come over for the funeral, to pay my respects, that's all.'

'Pay your respects, in what way?' We've already got two psychos running around, we don't need another one.' Debbie was never one to mince her words.

'I'm over all that now Debbie. I'm a changed man, I have a family.'

'Really Mickey?' said Daz. 'That's good to hear, even though I don't believe you. You wouldn't risk coming over here without a good reason. We all know exactly why you're here Mickey, to finish the job.'

'Eh, he hasn't threatened you two, has he?' I asked.

'No, not yet, but the word is that Peanut is after Ash, for his part in killing his brother, AK, as well as the missing drugs and money, that's why his dad ended up in the river. He couldn't get Ash, so he got his old man the poor bugger and his girlfriend,' said Debbie.

'The funeral is tomorrow, there won't be anyone there I expect, oh apart from Peanut who'll be on the prowl, probably looking for his next victim. Ash is in hiding and we are the only ones who know where he's staying,' Daz added.

'And where's that?' I asked.

'He's hiding out at his girlfriend's house,' said Daz.

'What, Ash has a girlfriend now?'

'Her name is Katie, you remember Katie?'

'His cousin Katie, you're kidding me. That's a bit…'

'It's his second cousin.'

'Well, I never would have thought they'd be an item, let alone live together. I bet I know who wears the trousers in that relationship. You said the funeral is tomorrow, where?'

'Nottingham Road, at two o' clock… but like I said, no one will be there,' replied Daz.

'You're wrong, I'll be there and so will Ash, I'll make sure of that.'

'You see, I was right, you're supposed to be bloody dead Mickey. In fact, your ashes are sprinkled on your brother's grave, we thought it would be a nice gesture.' Debbie replied.

'Mickey stay out of it mate, go back to Spain to your wife and kid, why do you want to risk all that. What if you get spotted?' Daz sounded nervous.

'Relax I won't be at the funeral I'll just be in the background watching Ash's back. I've thought and thought about it and I think the best thing to do is take Ash back to Spain with me.'

'And what about Katie, she might not want to go,' said Debbie.

'I'm not going to force them to come, I'll just suggest it as an option. Tell you what, I'll go and see them tomorrow morning and put it to them. If he says no, I'll just piss off back to Spain.'

I was talking bollocks, there was no great escape. I had other plans. I just wanted to stop Debbie worrying.

Daz and Debbie looked at each other without saying a word, then looked at me.

'Well, sounds like a plan to me,' said Daz

'Do you think I was born yesterday? You need to go Mickey; I don't believe a word you're saying.' Debbie knew me too well.

'Steady on Debbie,' said Daz

I got up to leave. 'It's ok I'll go. I understand.'

'It's 2am you can stay tonight, but tomorrow you've got to leave Mickey. I'm sorry.'

'Ok Debbie, thanks.'

'I'm driving into Derby tomorrow morning to pick the kids up so I'll drop you off near Katie's house. If you're going to the funeral you need to wear something decent and you can't go stinking like that.'

Debbie disappeared and reappeared with half a dozen of my old suits, some shirts, jeans and my old Canadian combat jacket. She had kept them from when we lived together.

'I thought you'd have thrown them out.' Given the circumstances of our last meeting I was surprised that she had kept anything belonging to me.

'No Mickey, I always thought you'd re-appear again one day. I just wish it could have been under better circumstances. Well, I'm off to bed, got a busy day tomorrow,' said Debbie, as she climbed the stairs.

I sat downstairs with Daz and talked about our old army days, purposely not bringing up the IED incident. We both knew that should be avoided at all costs, especially with my state of mind. I didn't need to be reminded of it.

'Mickey, you were talking bollocks earlier about going back to Spain with Ash, weren't you? Why would you want to come over here and risk everything? Are you still having those nightmares and stuff?'

I decided to tell him the truth about what had happened in Spain, it was hard to talk about it without welling up, but I told him everything.

'Fucking hell Mickey, I'm gutted for you mate, I knew there was a hidden agenda, do you want some advice from a mate? Hand yourself in Mickey, leave it to the Police. This all has to stop.'

'Not a chance,' I said.

There was a short silence. Daz knew he would never be able to change my mind, not a chance in hell of that. I needed my revenge.

So, what's your plan?' Daz asked.

'Peanut isn't the top of my to-do list right now. I need to find out who killed my Chrissie and I will not stop until I have. Do me a favour Daz, don't tell Debbie about this, will you.'

'No mate, she'd only worry even more, she still thinks a lot of you, you know. There isn't a day goes by when she hasn't mentioned you.'

'We had been through a lot together, me and Debs, she broke my heart when she sent me that 'dear John letter' whilst I was serving in Afghanistan, but she was only nineteen, we were all young back then. You have got a good one there Daz. Anyway, I need to get my head down mate, ready for tomorrow.'

'If there's anything I can do, if you need me, you know I've got your back.'

'Nah Daz, I can sort this out on my own and anyway look at the shit I got you into last time. You have Debbie and the kids to look after now.'

'Well, if you change your mind, just say.'

I gave my old friend a hug and I headed off for a shower, before hopefully having a decent night's sleep, in a proper bed for the first time in ages. However, it wasn't a good sleep, as I kept waking up every ten minutes.

The next morning, I woke up to the smell of frying bacon. I was soon down in the kitchen.

'Smells good, any of that for me?' I asked.

'It's all for you,' said Debbie. 'Daz only likes his cereal in the morning, don't you Daz?'

I sat down next to Daz, who was munching away at his bowl of sugar puffs while I was treated to a large fried breakfast, just like the old days. Debbie knew exactly what I liked.

A few minutes had gone by before anyone spoke. Then I started a conversation going.

'I heard sugar puffs stunt your growth Daz.'

Daz spat cereal all over the table.

'For fuck's sake Mickey, now look what you've made me do. That is not funny Mickey, I wondered how long it would take you to take the piss out of my disability, you wanker,' he said.

Debbie was not amused. She did not like dark humour.

'They are just absent without leave that's all,' I said

'They'll come back when they're ready won't they Mickey,' Daz replied.

'Ok, that's enough, you're both as bad as each other,' said Debbie. 'Right, I need to get ready. Hurry up and eat your breakfast Mickey, I'll take you into Derby once I'm ready.'

Half an hour later we were ready to leave. I said my goodbyes to Daz and mentioned I would be back to see him soon.

'Not too soon I hope,' said Debbie, laughing.

We pulled away and Daz waved us off from the doorstep. Debbie didn't waste any time laying into me.

'Please don't do anything stupid Mickey.'

'Like I said, I'm just there to make sure Ash sees his dad off, then I'll get him out of there.'

'But what if you get spotted?'

'I won't, don't worry, that's the last thing I want to do.'

It wasn't long before we hit heavy traffic, it was taking ages to get into Derby. I was soon fighting to stay awake. I struggled to keep my eyes open.

'Can I drive Debbie? I know you hate driving.'

'If you want to, Mickey.'

We pulled over and swapped seats, but not before she reminded me that we were not in Spain.

'Remember, it's the left side of the road over here.'

The road ahead was changing from two lane traffic to single lane and some idiot in a BMW came racing up the outside lane to get in front of us. I obviously would not let him in, he was now alongside me.

'Let him in Mickey!' Debbie urged me.

'No fucking chance, if he had indicated I would have done, but fuck him, he can wait his turn.'

I could see the guy going mental at me. I wound down my window.

'Have you got a problem mate?' I asked.

'Yes, you're the fucking problem,' he answered.

'Try indicating next time, you can't just barge your way in like that.'

'Fuck you,' he replied, giving me the middle finger.

'Mickey, let him in,' Debbie pleaded, looking worried.

'I'm not having it Debs; he thinks he's some sort of fucking big man.'

He didn't get his way and backed off, but it was not over and this idiot decided to tailgate me for the next ten miles down the A52. I even slowed down to 45mph in the inside lane, to let him overtake, but he stayed where he was and it was like this all the way to Derby. I went around a few roundabouts, but he followed me. This cunt had some sort of death wish.

'He's scaring me Mickey, who is he?'

'It's going to be alright Debbie, trust me.'

I decided to head for the local hospital, which was close by and not too far from the place where Debbie said she would drop me off. I entered the hospital's one-way system.

'What are you doing Mickey, why are we here?'

I turned off at the entrance to A&E, he was still behind me. I slammed on my brakes, and with an Ambulance behind him, he was trapped. I pulled my hood up over my head, got out of the car and walked towards his. I opened his car door and dragged him out. Two right hooks later and his head was bouncing off the bonnet, it did the trick, he was out of it.
I got back in the car and drove off, leaving my victim being attended to by hospital staff, Debbie didn't look too pleased.

'Sorry Debs but what else could I do, at least I took him to the right place, they'll look after him.'

'Bloody hell you haven't changed at all, low profile my arse! That place is crawling with CCTV.'

'Don't worry, I'll be long gone before they catch up with me.'

'What about me, Mickey?'

'Just tell them I hijacked the car, they won't know who I am, that's why I put my hood up.'

We drove on a short distance towards Katie's place and pulled over two streets away from her house.

'I'm sorry about that Debs.'

'You're awake then. Sorry about what? You've been asleep since we left the house,' she said.

'What about what just happened in the hospital?' I asked.

'Mickey what are you talking about,' Debbie asked, looking puzzled.

I looked at my knuckles, there were no cuts and I was not wearing a hoodie and not sitting in the driving seat. I dreamt the whole thing. Shit, the dreams were back.

'Mickey are you ok, still having those crazy dreams then, look why don't I pick the kids up and I take you back to our place for a few days, till you feel a bit better. Then you can travel home to your family, where you belong.'

'Belong? I don't belong anywhere anymore!' I said angrily.

I realised that I had upset Debbie and that was the last thing I wanted to do. Tears began tracing a path down her face.

'I'm sorry Debs, I didn't mean to shout. I'll be ok, I just need to see Ash, then I'll go home.'

Debbie gave me the directions to Katie's place. I leaned over and gave her a hug.

'Take care Debs.'

'And you Mickey, please, please, don't do anything stupid,' she pleaded, still crying. And they were her last words from the open window as she drove away.

I looked around to see if anyone was following me but there was no one around, only moving traffic. It was good to be back in Derby, even though I was here for all the wrong reasons. I soon arrived at Katie's house. I didn't go straight to the front door, I walked around the back, via the side entrance. I entered the back garden, sneaked up to the window and tapped on the glass. Hearing voices coming from inside, I tapped again.

'Who the fuck is that, Katie? I could hear the panic in Ash's voice.

'I don't bloody know, I'm not a mind reader,' Katie answered.

I tapped on the window again. 'Are you going to let me in or what? Ash, it's Mickey!' I said, in a raised voice.

The curtains opened a crack, before opening fully. Ash stared through the window at me, opened mouthed, then he opened the door.

'Oh my God, what the hell are you doing here? Come in, come in, Katie, it's Mickey. Put something decent on, Mickey's here. Shit, I didn't recognise you, what with the long hair and beard.'

It looked like Katie had just got out the shower and was wearing the shortest towel I had ever seen. I noticed straight away how much these two had grown up. Ash was the same size as me, he was now a fully grown man and Katie was an extremely good-looking young lady.

'Mickey you've turned up at the wrong time, you just don't want to be me, or anywhere near me right now.'

'Spare me the details, I know all about it. Why do you think I'm here?'

'Who told you where I was?' Ash asked.

'Never mind that, a coffee would go down well. Are you glad to see me?'

'No, I'm not Mickey, you need to be a million miles from here.'

'Not until you've been to your dad's funeral.'

'What! No way, I haven't got a death wish.'

Just then, Katie arrived back in the room and this time she was dressed.

'That's what I told him', said Katie. 'He has to go to the funeral. I don't know what you're worried about, even Peanut and Josh aren't stupid enough to turn up looking for you.'

'Maybe not, but they'll have their spies out, forget it, I'm not going,' he said, as he turned and walked out of the room.

'Well, I'll go on my own, then,' I called after him.

'I'll come too,' added Katie.

Ash came back into the room carrying three steaming mugs, which he placed on the coffee table.

'You've been back five minutes and you're stressing me out already Mickey, you're as bad as her.'

'Go to your father's funeral with Katie, I'll be there in the background just in case.'

Ash tried to defend his decision on not attending his father's funeral, although I know deep down that he wanted to say a final goodbye.

'It's not that I'm scared Mickey, it's just that I don't want anything to ruin what I've got with Katie. She is the best thing that has ever happened to me. Did you hear what they did to him Mickey? They slit his throat, bound him to his wheelchair and pushed him in the river.'

Katie was soon by his side, comforting him as he broke down in tears.

'Don't worry Ash, they've got it coming to them,' I said.

'You see, this is what I don't want Mickey. The Police told me they know who killed him but they're just not saying, so let them deal with it please.'

'What, like last time? Look at them now. Ash, go and see your dad off, nothing will happen to you, I promise.'

'Where have I heard that before? Why have you risked everything coming back here?'

'Because I heard my mate was in trouble Ash, so get ready and get it out of the way, then we can have a beer or two.'

Ash went quiet. I could see he was thinking about what I had said.

'Ok, but why do I have a bad feeling about this?'

I decided not to wear any of the suits that Debbie had given me, the last thing I wanted to do is stand out. The three of us took a taxi to the cemetery, which dropped us off a short walk from the entrance. Ash was nervous, visibly shaking, looking around anxiously, like a deer being stalked. Katie held his hand tightly.

'Off you go then Ash, go and see your old man off, you'll regret it if you don't go.'

'What about you?' Ash asked, as tears streamed down his face.

'Don't worry, I'll be close by. We'll meet back at your place later.'

They walked up the road to the main entrance, he was still looking around nervously, poor bloke. I could tell he was shitting himself. I remember having that feeling during my first time on patrol in Afghanistan and for good reason. Today, the difference between me and Ash was that he was worried that the evil bastard, who sliced his dad's throat open, would turn up to inflict further revenge. Whilst I was hoping that they would turn up, so I could inflict mine, but that would be being too kind to them. They needed to suffer, like the last time, but this time I'll stick around to watch and make sure the job is completed.

I made my way to a side entrance and took up position under the shadow of a few oak trees. I was surprised to see a congregation, though it was small, no more than twenty people. I didn't recognise anybody, the mourners were mainly older people. I scanned around the area to see if anyone of interest was watching the proceedings, well, the ones who I wanted to find that is.

At least Ash had got to see his dad off. Watching the funeral my thoughts soon turned to Chrissie and for a moment I got emotional. For fuck's sake, that is the last thing I wanted. I needed to concentrate on my surroundings. It was then, out of the corner of my left eye, I spotted two figures, my hand instantly moved to my pocket and wrapped tightly around my pistol grip and released the safety catch. Not so hasty Mickey, I thought to myself, it could be anyone, maybe press or coppers. Surely those two daft idiots would not turn up at their victim's funeral. I stepped back into the bushes and made my way towards them, making sure I could not be seen. I recognized one of them straight away, it was the landlord of The Anchor, the pub that AK used to own, but who was the other one? He had his hood up; he was too short to be Peanut, maybe someone reporting back to him, yes that must be it. After the burial, they turned to leave but I decided not to follow them. I stayed to protect Ash and Katie, but I had my link, I now knew where to start looking for Peanut and his friend.

Ten minutes later, after the funeral had finished, Katie walked back to where the taxi had dropped us off earlier and told me that a small wake had been organised by the local church, at a community centre nearby to where he had lived. I was invited, but I declined, worried I would bump into coppers or the press paying their respects, especially with it being a double murder, it was the perfect hunting ground.

'You're ok, I won't come in, but I'll be hanging around nearby just in case.'

But before that, I needed to do something. I could see Ash in the distance, he was looking a lot more relaxed as he mingled with the mourners, thanking them for coming.

'Thanks for doing that Mickey. I don't think anyone else could have persuaded him to come,' Katie said.

'It's ok, he would have come, even if it meant I had to drag him here.'

'I know,' said Katie, giggling.

'So, what now?' I asked.

'We've just got to keep our fingers crossed that the police catch the killers. Before you go, they don't know you're alive do they, Mickey?' she asked.

'I'm not alive though, am I? Go back to Ash, he needs you, tell him I'll be along in a bit, I need to visit my brother first.'

She didn't say another word, just reached over and kissed me on the cheek, smiled and walked away.

I popped into a nearby shop and bought four cans of his favourite beer and headed back towards the cemetery and to Matt's grave. It had been a couple of years since I last visited. The grave had been well kept, Debbie and Daz had been true to their word. I placed the beers in front of his headstone and stepped back. Usually we have a little chat, but not this time. All I could think about at that moment was the two of us as happy go lucky kids, full of life. I was remembering how upbeat and happy we both were, before joining up for the army on the same day. We were inseparable, until the day he was killed, that is when everything changed, it's been one big battle since then, trying to control the fear and aggression, always on the lookout for danger, the intrusive memories, nightmares and flashbacks. I thought being in Spain would be a fresh start and it was working, I was the happiest man alive, then it was all taken from me in an instant. There was too much going on in my head. I was an angry man. My brother being taken away, I had just about come to terms with that but now the only woman that I had truly loved and the mother of my little boy, was gone, I started to cry a little. Whilst staying on the yacht, I had blanked it out, but today, at my brother's graveside I had let go, I could hear Matt talking from his grave. '*So why are you standing there talking to me Mickey, get a fucking grip man, you have unfinished business, it is payback time.*' I had no need for the motivational talk, those fuckers are going to suffer and pay for what they did.

I left the cemetery and headed towards the community centre for the wake, doubling back a few times to make sure no one was following me. It was a long walk, about four miles, I had missed the wake and headed back to the house again. I entered from the rear of the property just in case they had any unwelcome visitors, or the property was being watched. It paid to be careful.

Later that evening, sitting in Katie's house, I caught up with Ash over a few beers. Katie had gone to bed, she had to be up early the next morning. She was a care assistant in a residential home around the corner from the house.

'Not a bad turnout in the end,' I said.

'No, I was surprised by how many people were there, people I hadn't seen in years and not a copper in sight, unless they were there in the background. It was Peanut and Josh that did it, I am sure of it. They failed to get at me, so they got my poor dad and Sandra. It wouldn't surprise me if Sandra sold my dad out, she set him up, but she wouldn't have known they were going to kill him, he was her fucking meal ticket.'

'I had a visitor over in Spain a few months ago.'

'Who?'

'Lisa.'

I waited to see if he would own up to telling her where I was.

'Sorry Mickey, she was desperate to find out where you were, at first I said I didn't know. Then she said that she needed help and that you always said if she was ever in trouble, you'd help her out.'

'I never said that.'

'Well, I assumed that with her and Colin saving our lives, it was true. So, she came over in the end, what did she want? I'm really sorry Mickey.'

'After I told her to sling her hook my Chrissie's boutique when up in flames…. with her and my son in it. Chrissie died in the fire but my son survived. He's staying with Chrissie's mum in London.'

Ash was lost for words, he looked like he was about to cry. 'I'm really sorry Mickey.'

'It wasn't your fault.'

I then spent the next half hour filling Ash in on what had happened since that horrible day.

'So, you see I'm not just here to take care of those two Muppets. I am here to find out who killed my Chrissie and I will. I'm sure that bitch Lisa had something to do with it. I did see someone I knew at the funeral, the landlord of The Anchor, that is if he still is landlord. He was with another bloke, but he was too small to be Peanut, I couldn't see his face. Why do you think they were there?'

'Scouting trip for Peanut?' Ash suggested.

'Who was the mystery guy,' I asked.

'The landlord's name is Nigel, the other one could probably be Colin,' said Ash

'Colin?' you mean 'The' Colin? AK's brother Colin? What the fuck is he doing back in Derby? He's supposed to have disappeared.'

'What, like you?' Ash replied. 'He never really left, Mickey, he spent a few months down in London but then he came back and he took over the drug deals that AK used to run, that is until Peanut and Josh came back on the scene. I think Peanut has ambitions of being top dog.'

'How do you know all this?'

'Katie, she doesn't miss much. She used to work for AK and Colin, dealing, remember? She's got her contacts. It wouldn't surprise me if Colin is shacked up at The Anchor.'

I decided not tell Ash, but I would pay The Anchor a visit in the early hours, to check out the lay of the land. I needed to figure out an entry and exit strategy.

'Where will you doss tonight, Mickey?'

'I was going to ask you if I could crash here on the sofa, just for tonight. I'll sort something out tomorrow.'

I could tell Ash was instantly relieved to hear me say that. It must have been a worrying time for him, knowing that Peanut could turn up any minute.

'Stay as long as you want mate, you're always welcome here... so, what's next Mickey?

'Operation fucking Peanut that's what's next, that cunt is walking dead, this world will be a better place once he and his mate are gone.'

Ash went off to bed. I lay on the sofa and tried to get some shut eye. I only managed a few hours before waking up in a cold sweat. It was thirteen minutes past two in the morning and I couldn't help but think that Peanut and Josh were out there somewhere, still fucking breathing. They could be anywhere. I needed to find them. I eventually fell back into a restless sleep. My plans of visiting The Anchor pub in the early hours were soon forgotten.

Chapter 6

I was woken up the next morning by the sounds of Katie getting ready for work. I pretended I was still asleep until I heard her leave through the back door.

For me, first thing in the morning had always been a good time for straight thinking. I needed a plan, and fast. I started thinking through my options, then Ash appeared, breaking my chain of thought.

'Morning, Mickey.'

'Fuck me, it's like Waterloo Station around here.'

'How do you like your tea?'

'NATO'

'What? Oh, I get it, it's a military thing, my dad used to say that.'

'NATO standard, white with two sugars. How come you're up so early?' I asked him.

'Couldn't sleep. I haven't been able to sleep since that day.'

'Don't worry, your problems will soon be over,' I said.

'Look, I've been thinking, Mickey, why don't I pack my case and fuck off with you right now, forget Peanut and Josh let the Police deal with them two.'

'Oh yeah, and what about Katie? Have you forgotten about her?'

'She'll understand. I am putting her life in danger too and anyway it won't be forever, just till it all blows over. I'll leave her a note, we can take her car, she won't mind.'

'And where do you think we're going to elope to Prince Charming?' I asked.

'Anywhere, I have some money stashed away.'

'Ash, can we change the subject.'

Ash went quiet. He could tell I had no interest in his plan. After a short pause, I changed the direction of the conversation. My mind had been working overtime while we were talking.

'Right, get me the biggest knife you've got, I need a little protection.'

'For fuck's sake Mickey.' Ash left the room and came back with a five-inch blade. 'It was my dad's fishing knife, you can have it.'

'The perfect revenge. Karma. I need some rope too, oh, and a hammer, I love a hammer.'

Ash looked on as I started to strip my pistol down to clean it. I needed to make sure it was in good working order.

I checked over the motley collection of weapons that I had accumulated and a hastily written list of other items that I needed. An hour later and I was ready, pistol, knife, rope, black nasty (masking tape) and a hammer, all hidden away nicely in my old Canadian combat jacket that Debbie had dug out for me. I put it on. It was like Doctor Who's TARDIS, everything was nicely concealed. Then I stood up and looked at myself in the mirror, for the first time in weeks and I didn't recognise myself. My hair was down to

my collar and my beard was out of control. I looked like
Saddam Hussain did when they found him in that hole in
the ground.

'Well, what do you reckon Ash?'

'You look like a homeless person, sleeping rough, no one
would guess you were a complete fucking psycho.'

'Perfect, well, time to leave Ash, I've got work to do.'

'That offer still stands you know. We can jump in the car
right now.'

'Say thanks to Katie for putting me up and I'll be in touch
soon, Ash. Stay out of sight for a few days and don't worry,
I won't be far away.'

I left the same way as I came, out the back door into the
garden and through the gap in the hedge which lead to the
main road. I headed towards The Anchor pub. I
remembered there was an old café over the road, if it is still
there it would be a great place to watch the comings and
goings. I was in luck, it was still there, exactly as I
remembered it and it had just opened for business.

'I'll have a cup of tea and a bacon sandwich, please,' I said
to the young girl behind the counter.

'That'll be five pounds twenty please, sit down and I'll
bring it over to you.'

I gave her the money and sat down near the window, where
I could look out through net curtains at the pub entrance.
The pub looked like it had had a revamp. An 'Under new
management' sign was posted in one of the windows, the
sign looked like it had been there for some time. There did
not appear to be much activity. The young girl placed my
mug of tea on the table, followed by my bacon sandwich.

'The pub over the road, it looks a lot nicer than it used to look,' I said to the young girl.

'Don't let that fool you, it's still a shit hole inside.'

'Do you know who the landlord is these days?' I asked.

'Same bloke as before I think. Not many people go in there, just the local idiots. I often wonder how it manages to stay open, it can't be making much money. Who are you anyway, another copper?' enquired the girl.

'No, I'm no copper, just a bloke having his breakfast.'

'They come in here all the time you know, just sitting where you're sitting, watching that place. I don't mind though as long as they're buying something.'

I sat there for another half hour pondering my next move, so do I just walk in there or wait till dark, I asked myself. After two more cups of tea and no activity apart from a postman delivering mail, I made my mind up I couldn't sit here all day. It would be safer to walk straight in there in broad daylight, rather than at night when the rats come out of their holes.

I said thank you to the young girl and left. I walked down the street for a few hundred yards, all the time checking no one was following me, then I turned around and headed back in the direction I had come from. I crossed the road and walked into the pub, both hands tightly gripping the tools of the trade that I had brought with me, just in case. I wasn't expecting any trouble, but you never know who you might end up bumping into. Entering the building, I could see the young girl was right, it was still a bit of a shit hole.

There were two lads playing pool but no barman or barmaid in sight. I approached the bar.

'Nige, you've got a customer!' shouted one of the lads who was playing pool. Suddenly, Nigel appeared.

'Yes mate, what you after?'

'Give me a pint of John Smith's please.'

'Here, don't I know you?' asked Nigel, pulling my pint.

'You might do, but not to my knowledge.'

The barman looked puzzled. I noticed the two lads playing pool did not take their eyes off me.

'I'm usually good with faces,' Nigel replied.

He handed me my beer, looking deep in thought. I went to sit down, near the door. The last time I was in here was with Ash, planning our little weed experiment, fucking hell that was one hell of a bad idea, it feels like I have come full circle.

'What you after mate?' said the smaller of the pool players, a scrawny little shit with ginger hair.

I thought it best to not answer him, so I ignored his question.

'Are you fucking deaf, I said what you after?'

Then the other one spoke, this one looked like he could handle himself, he was tall with a broken nose.

'Steady on Ginge, no need to be like that. You after some gear mate?'

'Nope. I've come in here for a pint. This is a public house, isn't it?'

Then I noticed the tattoo on the one called Ginge, which read MOB.

'Like your tatt,' I remarked, what does MOB stand for?'

'Money Over Bitches, that's what that means mate.'

I started to laugh; I just couldn't help it. What a fucking moron.

'Proper fucking gangster you are aren't you, sunshine,' I said, shaking my head.

'We've got ourselves a right gobby cunt here Merv,' he called out to his friend.

'Look mate, whoever you are, just drink your beer and leave, there's a good bloke,' said Nigel.

I looked around for any CCTV cameras, there were three, including the one behind the bar which was pointing straight at me. I made my first move.

'I've come to see Colin.' Fuck me, that grabbed their attention, they all looked at each other.

'Colin who?' said Nigel, frowning.

'Colin the guy who was with you at the funeral yesterday.'

'Are you a copper?' Nigel asked.

'Do I look like a fucking copper?' I replied.

The barman picked up the phone behind the bar. He turned his back to me as he made the call. Merv and Ginge stopped talking and looked towards the bar, as though they were waiting for their next command.

Upstairs, Colin was sitting, reading the paper and picking the horses he would be backing later that day, when the phone rings.

'Yeah, what is it, I'm busy.'

'Col, there's some guy who's just walked in and he's asking for you.'

Colin looks at the CCTV monitor and zooms in.

'Nope, I haven't got a clue who he is. What does he want? He looks like a smack head, get rid of him, tell him we're closed.'

'Ok.'

Ending his call, Nigel turned back to face me.

'Drink up mate, you're going.'

'Not until I've seen Colin.'

'Look, I've asked you nicely.'

'Tell him it's Mickey.'

While Nigel turned his back to pick up the phone again, the two lads turned towards me with their pool cues at the ready. Merv rested his hand on the table and leant over towards me and stuck the thick end of the cue under my chin, forcing me to look at him.

'Put the cue down and get your fucking hand off the table,' I said, through gritted teeth.

'He told you to leave, now fucking leave.'

'Fucking hell, I'm shitting myself and what are you going to do Rambo?' I was barely holding my temper in check.

'I'm going to beat the fucking shit out you, that's what I'm going to do,' Merv threatened.

'With one arm, now that would be a bit of an unfair disadvantage wouldn't it?'

'What you talking about? I ain't got one arm.'

Before he could say another word, the hammer I was carrying slid down the inside of my jacket sleeve and into my grip, then came crashing down on his hand, which was resting on the edge of my table. I have never heard such a high-pitched squeal. While Merv was rolling about the pub floor I was placing the hammer back in my side pocket. The other pool cue wielding maniac approached me on my right side, only to be stopped in his tracks by the sight of my fully loaded, well maintained pistol, pointing straight at his forehead.

'No you fucking don't.' I've never seen anyone run out through the door so fast.

'Looks like your back up has done a runner Merv.'

I was just getting started when Colin eventually appeared to calm things down.

'Mickey, I didn't recognize you, come on upstairs. Nigel, mop this blood up and I suggest you go and get a plaster on that Merv.'

'Plaster! He's bust my fucking hand Colin!'

'Fuck me, this is just like old times, M&M turning the place into a war zone again, put those toys away Mickey and come upstairs.'

I followed Colin upstairs. The room was basic, not a patch on the place he used to live in with his brother, it resembled a storage area with just the odd flash of expensive furniture. Colin caught me looking around the place, I was still wary that his brother would pop out at me from behind one of the units.

'Relax Mickey, there's only me and you up here, sit down. What would you like, brandy?' asked Colin.

'No, you're ok, can't stand the stuff anymore.'

Colin sat down opposite me and smiled, although I could tell he was nervous by the slight tremor in his voice as he spoke.

'Well, well, well, I had a feeling you'd turn up sooner or later,' he said.

'And why's that?' I asked.

'The small matter of Ash's dad, revenge, unfinished business should I say. I was at the funeral yesterday, sad day, very sad.'

'So, it was you then,' I said.

'You were there? I didn't see you,' Colin replied.

'I was standing right behind you, navy blue hoodie, black jeans, addidas grey trainers with blue stripes.'

'Fucking hell, that's scary. I take it you learned all about that in the Army, all that sneaking around. You could come and work for me Mickey, it'll be a vast improvement on those two morons downstairs.'

'What happened to your brother and his boyfriend Josh, don't they work for you?'

'You must be joking, those pair of loose cannons, they've been nothing but a pain since they got released.'

'They did it, didn't they?' There was no reply from Colin.

'They murdered that poor bastard and his missus didn't they.'

'That's why you are here isn't it, Mickey? Nothing would give me greater pleasure than to see those two disposed of.'

'But he's your own brother Colin.'

'So was fucking AK. I'm right though, aren't I, it's why you're here isn't it, why would you want to come back to this shit hole from Spain and risk everything?' How is Spain by the way, is it the perfect place to disappear?

'You still with Lisa?' I asked.

'No. We split up a couple of months ago. After what happened with AK, we had it all planned, we moved to London and rented a place for a while, well you know how much it costs to live in the capital, and what with Lisa's expensive life style, it wasn't long before the money ran out, so we started working for a right nasty bastard called Sali, trust me, you don't want to cross this guy, he make's AK look like a teddy bear, way out of our league. Then I found out she was shagging him, the dirty slag, but in a way he did me a favour. I had trouble keeping up with her, Mickey. I still see her now and then, strictly business, I definitely dodged a bullet with that one. The last I heard was that she'd moved in with him, she's his bitch now. So, I came back here and picked up where AK left off. Until those two came back on the scene.'

'How is business?'

'Business is good Mickey, I'm doing ok. You're lucky you caught me here, I only pop in now and again, I live somewhere else. Don't let the surroundings fool you, I like to keep a low profile. What is the point in flaunting it like my brother, where did that get him? It only creates jealous people and enemies,' said Colin, smiling.

Colin didn't fool me with his mister nice persona, this guy was just as evil as the brother he murdered. He carried on talking whilst getting up from his chair and disappearing behind some shelving, which made me twitchy. I reached into my pocket and gripped my pistol.

'And anyway, I have to adopt this lifestyle because I'm a wanted man, unlike like you. You're supposed to be dead. That's why I'm in a good position to make you an offer,' he continued, from behind the shelving.

Colin reappeared, carrying a bag, I loosened my grip on the pistol.

'I've made a decision Mickey,' he said, as he put the bag on the coffee table. 'That's for you.'

I cautiously peered into the bag; it was full of bundles of money.

'There's forty thousand in there, it's yours, but I want you to do something for me.'

'I'm listening,' I replied.

'Peanut and Josh, I want you to take care of them. As long as they're around causing mayhem nobody's safe.'

'Forget it Colin, you can keep your money, I was going to kill them anyway.'

'It's not all my money, half of it is what Ash gave me, he came to see me two weeks ago, frightened for his life. He knew that sooner or later Peanut would catch up with him, it was a payoff, that's why he's still breathing. He gave me twenty thousand to give to Peanut.'

'Wow, I've got to hand it to you Colin, I admire your honesty.'

'You know me Mickey, I'm not greedy, I've got enough money. In a few months I'll be out of the UK anyway.'

'Where are you going?'

'South America, I have a few friends down there. If I stay here, eventually I will get caught and I have visions of those two fucking it up for me, that's why I want them dead and I know that you will do a good job. I'll give you half now and the other half when the job's done.'

I sat back and took in what he was saying, why was he giving me forty thousand when I was going to kill them anyway. Something didn't make sense here.

'I still don't get it Colin, why don't you do it and keep the money?'

'Because I've already killed one of my brothers. I really don't think I could do it again.'

'So, where are they?'

'Scarborough, I told them to get out of Derby, it would only be a matter of time before the Police catch up with them. They're living in an old camper van that I bought off eBay, it's a right old wreck, it's white with red stripes on the sides. I doubt if there's another one like it still in existence.'

'Fucking hell, he could be anywhere.'

'I know exactly where he's at, he's at this place,' said Colin, handing me a business card SEA VIEW CLIFF TOPS HOLIDAY PARK. 'We all used to go there as kids. Peanut is quite fond of his sea fishing. You will probably find him on the rocks somewhere close by, he likes to go in the early morning. Josh is a lazy bastard, he'll spend most of his time in the van, shit faced. So, is it a deal?'

'Like I said, it was on my to do list anyway and who would say no to forty thousand.'

I zipped up the bag up after Colin had removed half the contents and stood up.

'Well, nice doing business with you Mickey and I wish you luck in your new venture,' said Colin, smiling.

'Fuck off Colin,' I said jokingly, while shaking his hand.

He shouted for Nigel, who ran up the stairs like he had been waiting for the call.

'See my friend Mickey out by way of the back door.'

I left The Anchor and headed back to Ash and Katie's house, carrying the bag of money. Well, I did not expect that, I thought. It didn't add up, why give me the money when he could have kept the money and done the job himself and I found it hard to believe him when he said he couldn't kill another brother. Maybe Colin was setting me up. Was the money to ensure I walked into a trap? He knows I'm not that stupid. Maybe he is just being a good guy, after all he did save my life once. I arrived back at Katie's house and knocked on the backdoor.

'Is that you Mickey?' Ash called out.

'Yes, let me in.'

'That was quick, did you find them?'

'No, but I know where they are now.'

'Where?'

'Is the offer still on about using Katie's car?'

'Yes of course, Mickey.'

Ash grabbed the keys out of a pot on the mantelpiece and offered them to me.

'Go and pack some stuff, we're leaving in ten minutes. Make sure you pack plenty, as we could be away for some time,' I told him.

I had no intentions of taking him with me, I had caused him enough trouble in the time I had known him. This job was for me alone. I planned to be long gone before he finished packing.

'But I need a shower?' Ash said as he headed towards the stairs.

'Well have a bloody shower then, just hurry up.'

Ash shot upstairs to have a shower and begin packing. I placed the money, less a few hundred pounds, on the coffee table and wrote a quick note.

'This is the money you gave Colin. He does not want it. I will bring the car back in a few days when the job's done… sorry not your fight. I quietly opened the front door and closed it behind me, climbed in the car and left. I did not like deceiving Ash like that, but it was for his own good, he had the chance of a future with Katie, which could be destroyed if he followed me.

Chapter 7

Scarborough, I was just a kid the last time I went there, we always stayed in a cheap guesthouse. Most days, my Mum and her latest fella would sunbathe fully clothed, sitting on hired deck chairs on a windy, chilly beach. While our mum and her bloke were trying to catch some sun, me and my brother, Matt, would hit the amusement arcades. I was about nine years old; my brother was seven. I would give the 'shove two pence' machines a good kick and the money would drop, the attendant would chase me round and round the arcade, while my cute, innocent, butter wouldn't melt in his mouth, little brother, filled his pockets to bursting with the coins. Partners in crime, we were close, very close, until the day he was taken away. I miss him.

I was driving a red mini, you could tell it was a woman's car, it smelt nice and it was clean, too clean. I knew I had to look after it or she would be on Ash's case. Katie was a strong girl, the perfect partner for Ash. I hope they stay together.

During most of the journey my mind was racing, thinking about the future, what next? I tried not to think about Chrissie and what could have been. I really do not think I would be around now if it wasn't for my son surviving the fire and the people that had helped me. I like to think that one day I'll be sitting on that windy Scarborough beach with my future partner, watching my kids enjoy their holiday, just like me and my brother did. I had been driving more than two hours and felt tired from lack of sleep. I began to feel depressed, my mind filled with dark thoughts, I needed to snap out of it. When it takes hold there is no warning. I began to cry as the weight of my thoughts crushed me.

I stopped in a layby to wipe the tears from my eyes. What is up with me, I ask myself, I can't stop reliving the events, having flashbacks of the past, but it is not just a flashback, I relive the whole thing. It always happens when I am alone for long periods or overly tired, like now. It was my fault that Ash's dad got murdered. If I hadn't had that argument with Chrissie which made her want to stay in the boutique that night she'd still be alive and if I hadn't taken that patrol route, my brother would be here now, sitting in the passenger seat and telling me to stop being a fucking cry baby and man up.

'I'm one, hopeless, worthless, piece of shit,' I said out loud, punching the steering wheel.

'No, you're not Mickey. You need to get focused, get rid of those negative thoughts and demons,' said Matt, who was sitting in the passenger seat. 'You were told to go on that patrol route, yes Chrissie died, but you didn't kill her, your son is still alive and you didn't slit Ash's dad's throat and push him in the fucking Derwent.'

I held on to the steering wheel tightly and looked straight ahead, hoping it was just a dream, that my dead brother was not sitting next to me in the car. I looked over again, he was still there, this time with the terrible injuries he had sustained in Afghanistan, an image I could never erase from my mind.

'Now get a fucking grip,' he said, angrily.

I turned away and looked straight ahead, eyes closed, heart beat racing, was this really happening? I turned to face him again, but this time he was gone. I was losing my fucking mind. I got out of the car, I needed to feel the ground under my feet. It is a war within me that never goes away. I can never escape from it because the walls are too thick and too tall now, with all the evil trapped inside. I began taking deep breaths, trying to banish the dark thoughts to the hidden places in my mind. It took me a while to come to my senses. The sign in the distance said Scarborough 36 miles, I needed to crack on and get to Scarborough. I was badly in need of a good night's sleep. I nervously got back in the car, started the engine and was on my way.

Arriving in Scarborough, I drove around for a while looking for a guest house close to the campsite but not too close, the last thing I needed was to bump into them. I soon found a place, it looked a bit of a dump but I did not come here for a holiday. I parked the car in a back street away from the guest house. I didn't want to leave a trail of evidence that I'd been anywhere near this place and there was a good chance Peanut and Josh would recognise the car, after all they'd been trying to find Ash for the last two weeks and not forgetting there was still a chance Colin could be setting me up.

I walked into the guest house; it was badly in need of a revamp. It was a dark and gloomy place, there was little daylight coming through and the air smelt of damp and boiled cabbage. I approached the reception.

'Can I help you, sir,' asked a middle-aged woman as she looked me up and down, frowning at my 'homeless person' appearance.

'Yes, I'd like to stay for a few days please.'

'And how many is a few days, it is Wednesday today, will you be wanting to stay over the weekend? We are fully booked up from Friday I'm afraid,' she informed me.

'Two days will be fine,' I replied.

'Single or double?'

'Err double.'

She looked past me, expecting someone else to be behind me.

'On your own, are you?' she asked.

'Yes, I like a big bed.'

'Oh, I see.'

I signed in, using a false name and address, paid her up front and was shown to my room, which was on the top floor. Walking up the stairs it was evident this place had been neglected for some time, wallpaper curled away from the damp walls and the stair carpet was full of bare patches. The receptionist opened the door, gave the room a cursory look and handed me the key. I closed the door behind me and walked towards the window, the view was great. I looked out over the rooftops of a number of similar Victorian buildings, taking in the sea view of the North Bay and the sound of seagulls flying overhead.

After making myself a coffee, I sat on the bed and turned on the TV, I wanted to just lay back and sleep, but I knew that was not possible, not just yet. It would be dark in an hour and I needed to go on a recce to find the camper van and some likely fishing spots. If I could achieve that I would be happy. There would be no fun and games tonight.

I needed a good night's sleep before I did anything, I needed to be switched on and ready.

I put my jacket on, pulled up my hood up and left the hotel, heading for the camp site about a mile away. Passing a few pubs on the way, I wondered if Peanut and Josh could be in one of them. I reached the camp site a short time later. It was a large site with one entrance, manned by a security guard. The site was mostly full of static caravans but somewhere towards the back was an area delegated for camper vans and tents. I walked round the perimeter a couple of times to get the lay of the land. I noticed a few holes in the fence, perfect easy access. At the rear of the campsite, facing the sea, was a sheer drop of about two hundred feet onto the rocks below, a poorly maintained, low wooden fence providing the only safety barrier. I walked around the site for a while before I spotted the van directly under a lamp post. It had to be their van, it was exactly as Colin had described it. There was no other van like it on the site, what a heap of junk. I didn't hang around, that was part one done, now for a quick walk along the front and back to the guest house.

The tide was now in, covering most of the rocks, so I couldn't see many places to fish from, but there would be lots of places to fish from along this coastline tomorrow morning, it was time to head back. I stopped at a fish and chip shop on my way, I realised I hadn't eaten all day. While I was waiting for my fish and chips to fry and be wrapped up, I heard two familiar voices behind me.

'Did you see his fucking nose explode, that was fucking hilarious?' Peanut said.

'That was sick, mate,' Josh replied.

I could not believe my ears. I stayed calm, so long as they didn't see my face, I'd be ok.

'Hurry up, I'm starving,' Peanut said to the guy behind the counter.

'That'll be £5.50 mate,' said the guy, as he served me.

I gave him the money without speaking, I just nodded at him and walked out through the door at the far end of the shop. Wow, that was close. What were the chances of that happening? I headed back to the guest house. On the way I passed a homeless guy. So that's who they were talking about. He was holding his nose whilst looking up at me. I knelt in front of him to see if he was ok, he flinched.

'It's ok mate, I'm not going to hurt you. What happened?' I asked him.

'Some guy just kicked me in the face. I only asked him if he had any change to spare.'

The bleeding began to slow down, then eventually stopped. I took out my fish and chips and gave him half on a piece of wrapping paper.

'There you go mate.'

'Thank you, thank you very much.'

'Listen, wrap that lot up and get away from here, it's not safe mate,' I advised him.

'Where would you suggest, I've got nowhere to go.'

I took forty pounds out of my pocket and gave it to him.

'I want you to leave now for your own safety,' I told him.

I didn't have to ask him twice. He quickly wrapped up his free dinner, took the money and wandered off into the night. I headed back to the guest house. I vaguely remembered seeing a sign on the wall outside the reception, informing guests that takeaway meals were not allowed inside the guest house. So, I hid what was left of my supper inside my Tardis of a jacket and smuggled it in. It reminded me of sneaking back into camp, past the guardroom in the Army. On entering the guest house, the landlady, who had checked me in earlier, was still in the reception area.

'Is the room ok Mister Bancroft,' she enquired.

'Err, yes, yes, thanks.'

'What is that smell' she asked, her nose twitching.

'Oh, I've just had fish and chips,' I lied, hoping to cover my tracks as I headed towards the stairs.

'Will you be having breakfast, Mister Bancroft?'

'Yes please.'

'Remember, breakfast finishes at 9am sharp,' she informed me.

'Ok, Goodnight,' I called back over my shoulder, as I climbed up the stairs.

It was nice to get back in my room, away from prying eyes. That was a close shave in the chip shop and that poor homeless guy, what had he done to deserve that? After seeing the state of his face, I felt like turning around and heading back to the chippie to empty my gun into them and fuck the consequences. I ate the rest of my fish and chips, watched a little TV and laid back on the bed, I was beat. The next thing I knew it was morning. It was the best sleep I had had for ages. After showering I went down for breakfast. There she was again. Did this woman ever stop? She was starting to piss me off!

'Did you have a good sleep, Mister Bancroft?'

'I certainly did Missus?'

'Mrs. Redford, but you can call me Jennifer. Can I get you anything else, more toast?'

'No this is fine.'

'So, what brings you to Scarborough, business or pleasure?'

'Business. I work in pest control.'

'Oh!! Well, you certainly will not find any pests in my guest house. May I ask what sort of pests?'

'Rats.'

'If you need anything, just let me know, I'll be in reception,' she said, scuttling away from my table in the dining room.

That got rid of her, the interfering old cow. For the remainder of the day I just rested, there wasn't much else to do apart from nipping over the road for a few snacks and the local paper. I needed to check the tidal charts to find out when the next high tide was.
I went to bed early that night. I set my alarm for 4am, before first light. The tide would be on its way in. With any luck Peanut will be casting his fishing rod off those rocks. I made myself comfortable and soon fell to sleep.

I woke up suddenly at 2am, I could feel cold metal being pressed into my forehead.

'Move and your dead for real this time, you cunt, turn the light on Josh,' said Peanut.

To my horror Peanut and Josh were standing either side of my bed, with sick grins on their faces.

'Fell for it, didn't you, Mister Dead,' said Peanut, grinning evilly

'Hook, line and sinker,' Josh said, laughing.

'My brother Colin set you up Mickey.'

'Done up like a kipper.'

'Shut the fuck up Josh.' Peanut was not happy at being interrupted by his sidekick. 'I thought you were cleverer than that, Mickey, but you're just a thick squaddie after all aren't you?'

He pressed the gun into my head even harder.

'Guess what Mickey, it's time to go back to sleep for good this time.'

I could see his trigger finger tighten on the trigger. I closed my eyes, waiting for the bullet that would end my life.

'Say goodbye Mickey, this is for AK.'

I shot out of bed, the room was dark again and my alarm clock was going off. The dream had felt so real. It took a while for me to come to my senses. I turned off the alarm and started to search the room to be doubly sure they were not there, that it was just a dream. I needed to calm myself down. I made myself a black coffee and got ready. Hopefully, this would be my last day in Scarborough. When I left the guest house the time was 4.15am. The conditions were in my favour, it was a very misty morning, visibility was about thirty yards. I could hear the birds starting to burst into song, but there was not a soul around.

I walked down the steep road that led to the sea front. I stood looking out at the exposed rocks. Peanut would be along here somewhere. The mist meant I could get really close to him before he spotted me, but I had to find him first. After walking along the sea front for five minutes the mist started to clear a little, it looked like it was End Ex, then in the distance, about a hundred metres out on the bare rocks, I could just make out a figure who was busy casting their line into the waves. It looked like it could be Peanut, my gamble had paid off. I walked towards him, being careful not to slip on the seaweed-covered rocks. I reached a point about ten metres behind him and just stood there watching him, it was Peanut. It must have been a few minutes before he realised he was not alone.

'Yes, what do you want, if you've come to tell me I can't fish here you're wasting your time and no I haven't caught anything,' he said without looking back.

I just let him babble on. I stayed quiet, observing his movements. I could have shot the bastard in the back, right there and then, and turned around and walked away, job done. No one would hear the gunshots, the crashing waves would muffle the sound, but no, I wanted him to know what it is like to suffer.

'Look mate, you're stressing me out, what's your fucking problem,' Peanut said, still intent on his fishing line.

'I haven't got a problem. It's you that's got a problem, a big fucking problem,' I replied.

Peanut turned round and strained his eyes to look at me. The colour drained from his face when he saw me standing there.

'It's you, I thought you were toast,' he spluttered, clearly shocked.

Peanut began to panic, he bent down, trying to find something in his backpack which was between his feet. He suddenly pulled out a large knife and waved it at me, smiling. I soon wiped the smile off his face when I produced my pistol, which I cocked and aimed at him.

'Did you really think I'd come all the way out here without being tooled up, you idiot. Drop the knife, drop the fucking knife,' I ordered him.

He released his grip on the knife, watching me as he did so. From the look on his face I could tell he was seething with anger. The knife landed with a dull clatter on the rocks before sliding into the sea.

'You need to be more careful Peanut, wandering around on the rocks in the middle of the night in this sea mist, anything might happen. Well, did you catch anything?'

He failed to answer me. I could see the warring emotions of anger and frustration flitting across his face. Peanut did not like being cornered. I watched as he gained control of his emotions before speaking.

'I haven't got any grief with you. Yeah, I cut off some of your mate's digits, but you cut some of mine off and you blew me up. I'd say we're more than even, there's no need for all this.'

I was just about to reply when my left foot slid down the side of the large rock I was standing on, I lost my grip on the pistol and watched with dismay as it fell into the sea. Before I knew it, Peanut was on top of me, he soon had me in a headlock.

'Not fast enough there, was you, soldier boy,' he said, grinning evilly.

He began tightening his grip around my neck. I knew I had to act fast, so I sank my teeth into his arm, which made him let go. I pulled my knife from my pocket and stabbed him. The blade went deep into his right leg, he let out a scream and fell backwards with my knife still embedded in his leg. He attempted to pull the knife out, intending to use it on me, but he was too slow. The large rock that I picked up crashed down on his head. He was now out cold. I looked around to make sure no one had witnessed the fight, that was the last thing I needed. There did not appear to be another person around and the mist had started to thicken again, which would make the next part of my operation easier to complete in secrecy. I dragged Peanut's limp body onto the beach nearby, then went back for his backpack, shovel, and bait bucket, kicking the remainder of his fishing gear into the sea. Moments later I was sitting down next to Peanut's unconscious body and wondering what to do next. Looking through his backpack I found his phone and a set of keys. It didn't matter how I killed him I still had to hide the body, so to save time I picked up the shovel and began to dig.

It was now 5.15am and the sea mist had thickened even more, visibility was around twenty-five metres. It took me some time to dig a hole big enough for the purpose I intended. I taped Peanut's ankles together and his hands behind his back, then dragged him into the hole in a sitting position and dropped a large boulder into his lap. Ten minutes later he was buried in the sand with just his blood smeared head and neck showing. He started to regain consciousness, I helped to speed the process up with a bucket of sea water.

'Morning,' I said, as he opened his eyes.

'What have you done, get me out, get me out of this hole you sick bastard.'

He attempted to shout for help, but I soon put a stop to that by putting the bucket over his head and letting him have his rant until he finally fell silent. I lifted the bucket off his head so I could speak to him.

'It's no good shouting, no one can hear you, are you going to be quiet?'

He didn't speak for a few seconds. I could tell he was trying to think of a way out of his current situation.

'Listen, how much do you want? I've got twenty thousand in Derby, you can have it, just get me out of this fucking hole,' he pleaded.

'Colin has already given me that as a down payment,' I replied.

'No, he hasn't. He wouldn't do that.'

'You're talking about the money Ash gave Colin, aren't you, hoping you would leave him alone? You'll have to do better than that.'

'Why would my brother give you that money, you're lying.'

'He gave me the money to kill you and your boyfriend. How the fuck would I know where you were, oh and another twenty thousand when the job's done. I could hardly believe my luck; I would have done it for free. Who would have believed it, your own brother wanting you dead? He must really fucking hate you, mind you, it doesn't surprise me after I witnessed him blowing the top of AK's skull off.'

'I don't believe you. He would never hurt one of his own family.'

'Well, you're never going to know now, not where you're going.'

'What are you going to do?'

I didn't answer his question straight away. I looked at my watch, took the tide table out of my pocket and checked it before replying.

'Me, I'm not going to do anything, it will be high tide in twenty minutes. Unless you're King Canute I reckon you're fucked mate.'

'Who's King Canute?'

'Didn't you do history at school, you know that bloke who told the waves to go back, wait a minute, forget it, I got it wrong, it didn't work for him anyway.'

'Please, I don't deserve to die like this,' Peanut said as he began to cry.

'Tell me, when you pulled that knife across Ash's dad's throat and then pushed the poor bugger into the Derwent, and killed his partner, did you really think you'd get away with it? You didn't give them a choice.'

'Fuck you.'

I took Peanut's phone out and started to take pictures with it.

'What are you doing?'

'I'm going to send these to Colin. You don't come all the way to Scarborough without taking any holiday snaps, well fucking smile then.'

'Please don't kill me, I don't want to die,' he sobbed.

'Oh dear, how sad, never mind,' I replied.

Peanut started to shout out, but the sound was suddenly stopped by his mouth filling with sea water. I watched as he struggled, without success, to raise his head above the water. I hung around for another five minutes until the sea had covered him. There was no feeling of remorse, he deserved to die like that, he was pure evil. Now for the other one. I put his mobile phone and keys in my pocket and left.

Walking back up the hill and along the coastal path I soon arrived at the camp site and gained access through one of the many holes in the fencing that I had discovered the night before. It was easy to locate the camper van, it stuck out a mile thanks to its red stripes. As I walked towards it, I could hear heavy snoring. I remembered what Colin had said, that Peanut liked his fishing, while Josh enjoyed his booze and sleep. Using Peanut's keys, I cautiously let myself in, holding my knife just in case, but I needn't have worried, Josh was sound asleep at the back of the camper, he didn't budge he just carried on snoring. I sat down at the small dining table, wondering what to do next. I could set it on fire! No, too many people around, there was bound to be at least one 'have a go hero' out there to put it out. I could just slit his throat! No that would be messy and too obvious. The sound of his snoring was starting to piss me off, no wonder Peanut fucked off fishing. Then it came to me, it was perfect, the perfect crime, it could even be classed as an unfortunate accident. I reached over to the driver's compartment and took off the hand brake and climbed out of the camper van, then I took away the chocks that secured the wheels. It was that simple. With the camper conveniently parked on a gentle slope, sloping down to the cliff's edge and the dodgy perimeter fence, all it needed is a bit of encouragement. With a little gentle persuasion, the camper van was on its way. I stood and watched the camper van as it gathered speed, rolling down towards the edge of the cliff, what made it even better is when a naked Josh appeared at the window with a puzzled look on his face, wondering what the fuck was going on. I was too slow with the camera but did give him a farewell wave as he disappeared over the edge to certain death, job done, End Ex. I took a quick look around me to make sure no one was about but it was all very peaceful. I made a quick exit from the camp site and headed for the guest house. It was just after 6am when I arrived back, there was just time for a couple of hours shut eye before breakfast and my journey back to Derby.

Entering the dining hall, I found it was now full of weekend residents. I found a table and sat down waiting for someone to take my breakfast order. I soon demolished a full English breakfast and a pot of tea before standing up and intending to leave. Missus Busy Body came bustling over to my table with her usual questions - did I enjoy my breakfast…was the room comfortable enough? I replied yes to both questions and said goodbye to the nosey old bat, but of course she could not let me leave without asking me one more question.

'So, did you manage to eradicate those nasty rats Mister Bancroft?' She asked, keeping her voice low so as not to alarm her other guests.

For a moment I thought she was talking about Peanut and Josh. She would be scared shitless if she knew the true nature of my work.

'Yes, job done, all of them killed stone dead,' I replied, smiling.

'Oh well, come back and see us soon, won't you.'

'I will, and if you have any more problems with rats give me a call,' I said as loudly as I could.

The noise of conversation in the dining hall stopped instantly, you could hear a pin drop. Her face was contorted with rage as she walked out of the room to go and hide in her little reception cubby hole.

I went back into my room to pack. Emptying my pockets, I came across Peanut's phone again. Looking through the messages, contacts, and pictures, there seemed to be a lot of interesting information. For a start, Peanut knew I wasn't killed in the fire at AK's house, but it's what I read next that brought me to my knees. My face burned with rage, I now had the answer, I knew who killed my Chrissie. That person was going to pay with their life. It took me a while to pull myself together after that revelation.

I left Scarborough, sticking to the country roads because I didn't want CCTV cameras tracking my movements, especially after what I had just done. What do I do now? It would not be long before the news got out about those two scum bags. I knew it would be wiser not to hang around in Derby for too long. I had come back to the UK to do a job, I had completed half my mission, now it was time to get revenge on Chrissie's killer.

I started to think of what I could do with the other twenty thousand, that's if Colin is being true to his word. I might send it to Chrissie's mother, Elena, for my son's upkeep. I was undecided, I would have to sleep on it.

It was early evening when I arrived back in Derby and pulled up outside Ash and Katie's place once again. I decided it would not be fair to ask to stay the night again.

After all, they were both safe now and they had their money back. I was the last person they would want in their life now. I got out of the car, posted the car keys through the letter box and went on my way. Maybe I will see them again one day, under better circumstances, who knows. I was happy for them; they made a great couple.

I didn't go straight to Colin's to collect my bounty, it would have to wait, I needed to disappear for a while, so I walked to the main bus station and jumped on a bus, it could have been going anywhere, I didn't care. Derby bus station was not far from the River Gardens, the very place where Andy and his partner had met their fate. The bus station had been modernized since my last visit, which was when I joined the Army, destination Litchfield Wittington barracks. I remember sitting on that bus like it was yesterday. I could see several other lads with the same slightly fearful facial expression. We were all roughly the same age. I wondered if any of them were heading for the same place. After a while someone broke the ice and my suspicions had been correct, all of us were joining up, the banter was good we were all now laughing and smiling, wondering what lay in store for us when we got there. This time it was just me on the bus, on my way to Burton upon Trent, about sixteen miles south of Derby. As soon as I arrived, I booked straight into the nearest hotel and that is where I stayed for several days, sleeping, resting, watching TV and planning my next move.

Chapter 8

After spending a few days at the hotel, I was going stir crazy, I had not left my room since arriving. The only person I had seen since checking in was the driver for the local takeaway. I turned on the TV to distract my thoughts. I didn't want to end up in the black pit of despair again, like I had on the yacht in Spain and on the journey up to Scarborough. There was a report on the news about two deaths, both in suspicious circumstances, in Scarborough. The report said Police were looking into a possible gang related double murder. The reporter didn't go into any detail about how the people had died, or their identities, but I knew who they were. I began switching from channel to channel but there were no more reports about the incidents, they must have caught whoever did it!

I lay there thinking to myself that once this is all over and I have no more enemies left to kill, do I head back to Spain and disappear again? Pep would find me a job, I'm sure of it. No, I don't think so, too many bad memories there, I couldn't go back. What about going to South America with Colin, not a chance, especially not now. I could hand myself in to the police, do the time and clear my name, after all what have they got on me…impersonating my dead brother, growing a few weed plants. So, I become a free man again and then what? Nah, it is too fucking late for that. I have seen too much shit. You can never just un-see shit like that. I could never be an insurance salesman now. It is too fucking late. I took out Peanut's phone and called Colin. He would not be expecting a call from his dead brother.

'... Peanut, is that you? Where are you?' Colin sounded anxious.

'No, it's Mickey, don't you watch the news?'

'Yes and of course I know who it is, but it could have been the police calling me, Mickey, don't forget I'm wanted too you know.'

'We're all wanted Colin.'

'Well, how did it go, did you have any problems?' Colin asked.

'It went well Colin, what can I say, do you want the gory details?'

It was then that I decided to send him the holiday snaps on the beach, so he could see how his brother had met his end.

'You're one sick fuck Mickey, you didn't have to do that, that's my brother remember.'

'I'm the sick one? You're the one who killed your own brother and paid me to kill this one. He got what was coming to him, which brings me on to the question of payment When do I get my money?'

'You can have it when you want. It's here waiting for you to collect it.'

'How about tomorrow? I need to move on, where are you?'

He would not tell me where he was staying. Colin suggested that we meet the next day, Sunday, at 11am, at a local landmark in Derby called the Racecourse, close to

Derbyshire cricket ground and a twenty-minute walk from the town centre.

'Make sure you come on your own,' I advised him.

'Mickey, what's up, don't you trust me? You sound angry, what's up?' Colin asked.

'Tell you what, I'll have a big fucking smile on my face just for you. Eleven tomorrow, bye.' I ended the call, not wanting to say what I really felt like saying to him.

Sunday morning, around nine thirty, I got off the train at Derby station, this time I did not come tooled up, all I had on me was Peanut's mobile. I was confident nothing was going to happen. My intention was not to collect the twenty thousand and not to meet Colin, it was to find out where he was staying. I now knew who had killed Chrissie, it was Colin and his slag of a girlfriend, Lisa. The messages on Peanut's phone did not lie. I scrolled through the messages again.

Colin: 'There's no need to worry about Mickey, the cunt is toast.'

Peanut: 'That's really sad to hear Bro. Sadly, I wasn't there to see him burn.'

Colin: 'Make sure you delete these messages.'

Peanut: 'Stop fucking flapping, I always delete your messages.'

The date of the message was the day after the fire that killed Chrissie, that's why Peanut said to me on those rocks, 'I thought you were toast.'

I arrived early at the Racecourse. The place was busier than I thought. What used to be a Racecourse, before WW2, was

now a recreation ground and a venue for the amateur
football clubs who played their matches there on Saturdays
and Sundays. There must have been at least a dozen
matches taking place that day. I walked along the line of
trees, trying not to be seen, then I spotted him in the car
park, at the burger van, he was carrying a sports bag. I got a
little closer to confirm it was him and it was. I darted
behind some wooden fencing. It was time to give him a
call.

'Colin.'

'Mickey, where are you?'

'Listen mate, I got off the train at Derby station, started
walking and noticed two guys following me. They're not
your guys, are they?'

'Why would I do that? You need to chill Mickey, I have
your money here, come and get it.'

'We'll have to make it another time, they might be coppers,
I'll be in touch. Don't spend my fucking money will you.'

Colin laughed 'Mickey, it'll always be here.'

'Ok, I'll contact you in a few days.'

I was never going to collect the money that day nor get my
revenge, not yet. I just needed to know where he was
hiding out. I followed Colin as he left the Racecourse car
park and into the housing estate. I knew the area quite well
so I could keep my distance without losing him, he looked
around a few times but did not spot me, then after ten
minutes of walking he turned up an alley. The alley lead to
a row of eight houses. I could not get close enough to see
which one he had disappeared into. Now I was sticking out
like a sore thumb. I decided to leave and come back when it
was dark. Just as I was about to turn and go, I struck lucky.

A car pulled up and out stepped Merv, with his arm in a sling, and his brave side kick, Ginge. They both entered the third property down from the alley. So, now I knew where Colin was hanging out. That was all the information I needed. A quick look at online maps would give me the house number.

Walking back to the station I thought hard about my next move. But there was one thing that was puzzling me. So, their intention was to kill me, but they killed Chrissie by mistake, no wonder they had a big shock when I turned up. Why would he want me dead, I just didn't get it? This is the same guy who saved my life when his older brother AK had been intent on killing me. Was the twenty thousand guilt money for killing Chrissie? As I was walking down the main road nearing the station, my questions were about to be answered. A car pulled up beside me and two males jumped out and confronted me.

'Mickey, we meet again, fancy seeing you here,' one of them said.

I recognised him straight away, it was the random guy I met in Pep's bar, the one who claimed we served together in the regiment. I had last seen him around the time Chrissie died, this was all I needed.

'We need to have a little chat Mickey.'

'I don't think so, get out my way.'

He took out his police ID and waved it in front of me. I should have guessed they were coppers.

'I'm Detective Sergeant Bryant and this is Detective Constable Tully, we just want a chat Mickey, that's all, won't take long.'

'What if I say no?'

'Then we'll have to arrest you I suppose and take you to the station. I am sure you do not want that, do you? So, what's it to be?'

I had no choice but to climb into the unmarked car, is this it, is this where it ends. What have they got on me? I wished I had taken Colin out now. Shit, I still had Peanut's mobile on me. I managed to slip my hand in my pocket and turn it off.

'Where are we going?' I asked.

'Oh, not far, chilly day today, I bet you wish you were back in the sun. Do you miss it?'

I didn't reply, I just stared out of the window watching the world go by. I wondered what they wanted from me. Did they know about Scarborough? I don't think so, if they did, I would be on my way to the local nick and we were heading away from that. I settled back in the seat and waited to find out where the journey would end.

Ten minutes later we pulled into the car park of The Ragley, a pub and steak house, situated on the outskirts of Derby. With a copper on each side of me, we all walked in together. Bryant went to the bar while Tully escorted me to a seat. Minutes later we were all sitting in the far corner of the restaurant. A waitress delivered three coffees to the table.

'Well, this is nice isn't it?' Bryant looked me straight in the face as he took a long drink of his cappuccino.

'What is this all about, you said you could arrest me, what for?'

They both gave me an incredulous look.

'Bloody hell Mickey, do you really want us to tell you?' Bryant shook his head as he spoke.

'All I did was use my poor departed brother's identity and grow a few weed plants, for fuck's sake, that's hardly the crime of the century.'

'It was more than a few, Mickey, average street value of approximately three hundred thousand they reckon.'

'Don't you read the papers, I was being blackmailed into growing it remember.'

'Is that right?'

'Look, you either arrest me or I'm walking out of this pub right now and you better start calling for back-up because you pair of Muppets are not going to stop me.'

'Calm down Mickey, there's no need for that, we don't want to arrest you. We want you to help us'

His tone was a little more laid back. I wondered what his angle was. What did he want from me?

'I was sorry to hear about what happened to your partner, Chrissie.'

If his tactic was to calm me down, he had started off on the wrong subject, I did not speak.

'The Spanish police did want to speak to you, but now they want to speak to this man in connection with the fire that caused her death.'

Tully placed a still of a CCTV image down on the table.

'You know who that is don't you?' Bryant said.

The image was of Colin getting out of a car on the street where Chrissie's boutique had been, if I had not been one hundred percent certain that Colin was Chrissie's killer then the proof was right there in front of me. Bryant saw my reaction. I was an angry man.

'I know who that is, that's a dead man walking,' I replied, trying to control the anger building up inside.

'The Spanish police have the evidence that he killed Chrissie and there's an international warrant out for his arrest.'

'So, what now? You should be out there trying to find him not wasting your time with me.'

'We don't know where he is, do you?' Bryant asked, raising his eyebrows as he spoke.

Now I had a choice to make. I could tell them where he was, but what would happen? If he does get arrested and charged, the most a judge will sentence him to is a twelve year stretch, released after eight, for manslaughter. He could even walk free, like Peanut and Josh, no way, I could never let that happen, this cunt was going to die like his brothers.

'Haven't got a clue,' I replied, pushing the picture back towards Tully. 'All I'm saying is you better find him first.'

'Mickey, you disappoint me,' Bryant said.

'Hold on a minute, you had no problem in finding me, why can't you find him. He was at Ash's dad's funeral the other week if you'd cared enough to look for him.'

The two policemen looked at each other, both clearly surprised by my comment.

'We missed that one,' said Tully, looking perplexed.

'That was the last time I saw him. I was hiding in the tree line at the time. I wish I'd known then what I know now,' I answered.

'We only saw you, Mickey, after you spoke to Katie. Then you paid your respects to your brother at his graveside,' Bryant replied.

'So why didn't you pull me in then?'

'We didn't want to because we thought you'd lead us to Colin, then we lost you again. Bit of a slippery character aren't you,' Bryant added. 'Where did you disappear to? You have been off our radar for a few weeks. You didn't by any chance take a trip up to Scarborough, did you?'

'Why the fuck would I want to go up there?'

Tully placed two more images in front of me, they were of Peanut and Josh.

'Have you ever seen these two before?' asked Bryant.

'No, and I wouldn't want to either, they look a right pair of inbreeds.'

'The guy on the right was found buried up to his neck on the beach with a mouth full of crabs, you wouldn't know anything about that would you? The other one here decided to drive his camper van over a cliff onto the rocks below.'

I tried not to laugh at Bryant's description, but failed to stop the smile from spreading across my face.

'So, you've never come across these two before?' Tully probed.

'No, never.'

'You're lying Mickey, I know you are lying, come on, we're not in the station. They are Peanut and Josh, we know you've met up with them before. If you remember, you tried to blow them both up.'

'Well, if you know that already, why are you asking me?'

'Why did you come back to the UK, Mickey?'

'To find out who killed Chrissie, that's all I was interested in, and now I know, so stop wasting your time on me and go and find him.'

'It's not just that though is it Mickey, you also wanted to get revenge on the killers of Ash's father, didn't you?'

'Are you asking me or telling me. Is that it? I have told you what you want to know. You said just a few questions, I'm sorry but this doesn't look to me like a police interview room, unless they're serving up 8oz sirloin, or T bone steaks in the station these days'

Before I could say another word, Tully placed another picture down on the table.

'I guess you know who she is,' Bryant said.

'Lisa, Colin's other half. Have you arrested her yet? She was part of it, I'm sure.'

'That's where you're wrong, Mickey.'

'Where is all this going? I thought you said you wanted me to help you.'

Bryant took another sip of his cappuccino before explaining how he knew Lisa had not been involved in the fire that had killed Chrissie and what he needed from me.

'Lisa was Colin's girlfriend until she found out he was responsible for the fire that killed Chrissie. After the fire at AK's house, Colin and Lisa disappeared to London with what was left of AK's money. Before long they met up with AK's supplier, a guy called Sali, the leader of an Albanian crime gang. Colin and Lisa became good friends with Sali and it wasn't long before Colin became Sali's right-hand man and the main courier and major supplier of heroin into the midlands to three major gangs. Everything was going smoothly until Colin found out that Sali was getting a little too interested in Lisa. So, the pair decided to walk away and set up again where AK had left off back in Derby, hoping to muscle in on Sali's contacts abroad. That's why Colin and Lisa arrived in Spain to ask you to help them, hoping you would know some contacts, but her charms didn't work and you sent her packing, which didn't go down well with Colin. We know Lisa flew back to the UK the day before the fire, so we know she was never involved directly with Chrissie's death. Colin came back the day after the fire. When Lisa found out that Colin had started the fire, she came to us and told us everything, including what happened that day when AK was killed. How are your teeth by the way?'

When he said that, it was obvious he knew everything, he was not bullshitting me. I sat and waited for him to continue.

'She also told us how Colin blew his own brother AK's brains out in the back of a van. It would not surprise me to find out that it was Colin who killed Peanut and Josh. My guess is that he's cleaning house.'

Bryant's last comment proved he didn't know everything, which was fine by me. At least I knew I would not be facing a murder charge any time soon.

'Mickey there is something happening here which is much bigger than all this. Let me explain why we brought you here today and why we need your help. We and the

National Crime Agency have had Sali and his co-conspirators under Police surveillance for months. Sali is an Albanian drug kingpin and at the helm of a multi-million-pound cocaine racket, which he runs from his base in London. They are a sophisticated and organised criminal group, they receive large quantities of cocaine at the point of importation and manage the wholesale distribution across the UK to other organised criminal groups. These scum bags are making millions on the back of others misery. Stopping criminals like these, who care nothing about the damage they are causing in communities or the children they are exploiting by County Lines drug dealing, is our absolute priority. We suspect these men were involved in an industrial-scale operation, one the biggest ever uncovered in the UK. We have been monitoring Sali for months but we do not have quite enough information, we just need that final piece of the jigsaw. We need to know how the drugs are coming into the UK, the supply route and where they end up.'

'Where does Lisa come into it, where is she now?' I asked, when Bryant finished speaking.

'She is helping us.'

'But where is she, how is she helping?'

'Lisa is Sali's girlfriend.' Bryant informed me.

I started to laugh. 'That sounds about right. And she's also working for you.'

'Correct. The problem is that so far she can't get any information out of him, he's too clever for that.'

'So how do I fit in with your plans?'

'Sali knows of you already and your reputation as a person not to be messed with. He knows you are supposed to be dead, a fugitive. He also knows you refused to help supply Colin, thanks to Lisa. She is going to ask Sali to give you a job in his gang, he won't suspect anything, he needs people like you around him.'

'Thanks for the CV, it's flattering. So, you want me to find out everything I can about Sali and his network and how it's coming in.'

'Yes, and the pickup point.'

'And what do I get out of it?'

'We'll offer you the same deal as Lisa. If you can help us smash this gang, I'm sure you will be able to walk away a free man. Come on, surely you don't want to carry on living your life like this do you? Live a normal life, see your little boy. Come on Mickey, that is what you want is it not, to get amongst it. Pretend you're going into a war zone against the Taliban.'

I sat thinking about what he had said, it would be nice to live my life without constantly looking over my shoulder, but a couple of words made me doubt what he was offering.

'You said 'I'm sure'… that sounds like you're talking bollocks,' I said.

'Look, I can't promise you your freedom, but if you do this it will help. Think of the boy.'

These guys were unaware that I knew exactly how and when the drugs enter the UK. What time, what port, even what they are hidden in. I even knew they were accompanied by thousands of plum tomatoes. I know where the pickup point is and if they were lucky, along with the drugs, they might get the odd assassin, fugitive, illegal immigrant or terrorist! I suddenly remembered the address that Yakubu had gotten me to write down, I needed to tell them about that. They knew and I knew that I never really had a choice, it was either go with it or get arrested and be stuck on remand for six months. But to be honest, it sounded right up my street. I was in.

'I tell you what, count me in, but these are my demands. I need money to buy some new clothes, I can hardly turn up looking like a fucking member of the great unwashed. I also need a car to get back to Burton-on-Trent.'

'We'll do our best Mickey.' was the only reply I got from Bryant.

'By the way, on my way over here I came across some information, some bloke I met was eves dropping on a conversation, it's an address for a possible terrorist safe house in Manchester, don't ask me for more information because there isn't any.'

I handed him the scrap of paper with the address on it that Yakubu had heard mentioned.

'How reliable is this?'

'I don't know, it's up to you to find out, you're the copper. Right, how about a nice steak, I'm starving.'

I didn't get my steak or a car, just money to sort myself out and a burner (cheap phone, pay as you go) so they could contact me. But they did give me a lift back to my hotel. Even though I had said yes to their offer I was already having second thoughts. Did I really want to get myself involved in all that shit when I could take Colin's twenty grand and disappear again? I decided to sleep on it.

The next morning, whilst still in my room, I sat staring at my little boy's picture in my locket. I was so glad he was in safe hands, far away from all this. The mobile phone I had been given began to ring, it was DI Bryant calling to give me my instructions. I had no choice, I had to do this for my boy. If there was any possibility I could eventually lead a normal life, if there is such a thing, I had to go for it. The instructions were simple, I was to meet up with Lisa at 2pm at London St Pancras station on Friday, today was Wednesday. My mind was made up, I was in for the ride. It was time to call Colin for the last time.

'Mickey!' he sounded like he didn't have a care in the world. 'I think I know why you're calling, you want your money I take it.'

'Yes, but there's a problem, I need to get out of Derby because I think they're on to me.'

'Who?'

'Who do you think, the pigs. I'm sure I was being followed the other day at the Racecourse, unless I'm losing it, anyway, I thought it might be best if I lay low for a few weeks.'

'That's a pity, I was going to offer you a job.'

'A job. What sort of job?'

'Come on Mickey, a man with your skills, I'm sure I can put them to good use. I've got a job that's right up your street, down in London.'

'Nah, you're ok. Listen, I want you to do me a favour, that twenty grand, well, I've decided I'm going to donate it towards my son's future, it's the least I can do.'

'Nice touch Mickey. So, you are human after all.'

At that moment I had to bite my lip. The cunt has got a nerve. I gave him a forwarding address to send the money to.

'I'll get if off first thing tomorrow morning.'

'Make sure you do, or I'll be paying you a visit,' I replied.

Colin started to laugh. 'Mickey, trust me, your money will be sent.'

'Good.'

'Oh, by the way, what are you going to do with that phone you're calling me on? Peanut's phone.'

'Don't worry, it's the last time I'll be using it, I'll destroy it. I mean with all that information on it you wouldn't want it getting in the wrong hands, would you?'

This time there was no laughing. 'Like I said, your money is as good as there.'

'Ok, I'll be in touch.' I didn't give him the chance to answer and ended the call.

I stayed in the hotel for one more night before leaving for Derby. I wanted to say my goodbyes to Daz, Debbie, Ash and Katie. I was unsure whether I would survive my next mission. I went to see Daz and Debbie first, luckily, they were both at home. I was surprised at how emotional Debbie got when I told them, it would probably be the last time they saw me. I made my excuses and made a quick exit. Ash looked a lot more relaxed than when I had last seen him, obviously he had seen the reports about the demise of Peanut and Josh. We spent a few hours drinking beer and talking about the past. Ash was the only person, other than Colin and Lisa, who knew what AK had put me through before he was killed. Having had one too many beers I spent the night on Ash's sofa. It felt strange, for the first time since I arrived back in the UK I could finally relax because no one was trying to find me and I wasn't looking for anybody, but I knew this would all change the following day.

Chapter 9

I caught the 11.35 am train from Derby station, a trip I used to make regularly when visiting Chrissie. I wish I could turn back the clock. Just before the train pulled away a familiar face got on and sat down opposite me.

'Mickey, how are you? I see you didn't bother spending any of that money we gave you. You could have at least shaved that beard off and bought some decent clothes.'

Why was he always so fucking cheerful? It was Bryant being his usual happy self. He was probably checking to make sure I was on the train as planned.

'I thought I'd wait until I arrived in London seeing as you lot are splashing the cash. Oh, and you can take your phone back, you can keep your death warrant. I have no idea what I will be walking into. My guess is our Eastern European friends will be quite partial to dishing out some serious violence.' I shoved the phone towards him.

'So how are we going to communicate with you, Mickey?'

'Don't worry, I'll find a way and anyway I've already memorized your number. What was it you wanted to tell me?'

'Nothing really, I just wanted to wish you luck that's all.'

'You mean you wanted to make sure I was on the train. I'd advise you to get off now, this train leaves in sixty seconds.'

Bryant stood up, getting ready to leave the train.

'I mean it Mickey, good luck fella.'

Now there was a word I had not heard for a while. I shook his hand and he got off the train. I waved to him as the train passed him on its way out of the station.

The train arrived at St Pancras slightly early, they didn't tell me where she would be waiting, I guessed she would be on the platform but I guessed wrong, there was no sign of her. I knew she would not be hard to find, there were only a few places she could be.

It wasn't long before I spotted her, she was sitting elegantly at a glass table outside the coffee shop, busy tapping a message on her mobile phone and sipping her Americano. I have got to be honest, Lisa was a beautiful woman, with immaculate dress sense. I carried on watching her for a while, scanning around to see if she was on her own, which I doubted. She was the boss's bit of stuff, so she would be protected and I wasn't wrong. About twenty yards away stood a guy who was pretending to read a newspaper, looking at him, he definitely wasn't the type to be reading the Guardian for fuck's sake. I walked over to her table; she took a quick glance at me as she continued to text.

'Sorry I haven't got any money to give you,' said Lisa.

'Lisa it's me, Mickey.'

'Oh my god, you look terrible. I thought you were…'

'A dosser, I am, I suppose. Do you mind?' I said, pulling out the chair opposite.

'No, of course not, do you want a drink?'

I sat down 'No, I'm ok. I see you've brought your friend with you.' I inclined my head in the direction of the guy I'd spotted.

'Oh him, he's terrible. I tell you what, Mickey, some of the guys that Sali has working for him are a joke, honest. Try not to look at him, just play the game. I'm sorry about Chrissie, really sorry, as soon as I heard what had happened I went straight to the Police, honestly I had nothing to do with that.'

'If you say so Lisa, what's done is done, now change the subject.'

'It's good to see you. How are you now?'

'Change the subject.' I was determined to keep our relationship on a business level. I did not trust Lisa, no matter what Bryant said.

'Ok, strictly business yeah?'

'Yes.'

'What did Bryant tell you?'

'He filled me in on what they know about Sali and his set up and what they want me to do.'

'Sali might ask how and when I contacted you.'

'That's easy, I'll just tell him you contacted Ash, like you did when you wanted to find out where I lived in Spain.'

'Mickey you need to know that Sali is a clever guy, he doesn't trust anybody, not even me.'

'I don't blame him,' I said.

That angered her a little. She stood up and drank the rest of her coffee in one swallow.

'Come on, it's time to go,' she informed me.

We headed for the underground station and took a tube to Camden town, her body guard sat a few seats down from us. We carried on our conversation on the tube.

'So why did you agree to do this?' I asked.

'The same reason you did probably, plus I had no real choice. I just want out of this life. You look a bit rough by the way.'

'Thanks. What's that shit you've got on?'

'Is that the best you can do for a chat up line? It's 'Bond no. 9' by the way, costs a grand a bottle. Sali bought it for me from Harrods.'

'Drug money then,' I said.

She gave me a withering look before replying.

'I can't believe I actually wanted to fuck you a few months ago.' She shook her head at the memory.

'I'm flattered,' I replied.

'You need to smarten yourself up for tonight Mickey. Do you need any money?'

'No. I've got money.'

We soon ran out of nice things to say to each other and sat in silence until the train stopped at Camden town. A short walk from the station we arrived at an electrical shop, to one side of the shop entrance there was a door leading to a first-floor apartment above the shop. Lisa took out a key and opened the door. A flight of stairs lead up to the apartment above. We quickly ascended the stairs, only to be confronted by another door.

'This is where you'll be staying, it's all yours for the time being,' she said, unlocking the second door.

'Very nice,' I replied, taking a cursory glance from the doorway.

I had a brief tour of the apartment to check for any weak spots, it paid to be cautious. Once Lisa left, I would check for any listening devices. I didn't know how sophisticated the gang's methods were and I was taking no chances. The apartment was surprisingly smart and stylish. It had a bright modern kitchen and a luxury bathroom, which had a marble floor and Jacuzzi bath.

'This is where me and Colin stayed when we were together. I hate the place now. Make yourself at home, there's fresh food in the kitchen. Someone will pick you up around 7.30 pm, they will pull up outside the shop and pip the car horn twice. Any questions? she asked, as she handed me the key. 'Oh, and by the way, the shower works,' she added, smiling, before shutting the door behind her.

She had to have the last insult. I could tell it was going to be an icy relationship, but I knew we would have to get serious if this was going to work. The first thing I did after she left was to make myself a coffee and a few slices of toast. I sat chilling on the white leather sofa, munching away on the toast. The apartment looked out on the approach to the station entrance. Great for getting in and out the city, I bet this place was worth a few quid.

I left the flat an hour later and headed for the shops, destination barber. One hour later I left the barber's feeling like a newly sheared sheep, now it was time to buy some new clothes. Walking round the shops I noticed a short, stocky guy walking slowly behind me. After a while of popping in and out of different shops he was still there. I decided to double back and walked towards him, he changed direction and stopped at the bus stop and adopted the 'I am waiting for a bus' pose. Where the hell did Sali get these guys from? I walked on a few hundred yards and headed down a side street and waited for him to appear. As he came around the corner, I pulled him towards me and pushed him against the wall.

'Who are you?' I said. 'Who the fuck, are you?'

'Let me go,' he replied.

'Not until you tell me who you are.'

He started to struggle and lashed out at me. A short, sharp punch to the throat calmed him down, the problem now was that he couldn't speak even if he wanted to. As I was about to search his pockets, an old woman with a dog appeared which took me by surprise. I loosened my grip and he managed to run off. I brushed myself down and picked up my bags.

'Are you ok dear? You need to be careful around here, there's far too many bad people you know,' the old woman said, looking concerned.

After assuring the woman that I was fine, I retraced my steps and headed for my temporary home. I arrived back at my new apartment, still puzzled about who he could have been, maybe he wasn't one of Sali's men. After a short snooze, I got myself ready. So, this was it, I get to meet the boss. I wonder if we will hit it off, or could I be walking straight into a trap. Lisa said he was looking forward to seeing me but I had to be on the ball. People like Sali do not become gang bosses for being nice. With millions of pounds at stake I'll be swiftly dealt with if he sniffs a rat. At 7.30 pm on the dot I heard the two blasts on the horn and headed downstairs.

'Mickey?' enquired the driver.

'Yes. I'm Mickey.'

'Jump in.'

He drove for about four miles before he dropped me off outside a Chinese restaurant called the Shing Do. I entered the building cautiously and was greeted by Lisa. She looked me up and down as though she was inspecting me.

'Now that's the Mickey I remember, follow me and I'll introduce you to Sali.'

Before we went any further, I was searched by one of Sali's men, name of Bledor, who I later discovered was Sali's older brother. I was expecting it. All I had on me was Peanut's phone, which he stripped down and put back together again before handing it back with a smile. Lisa then lead me down a corridor towards the rear of the restaurant. At the end of the corridor were two doors, one to the left and one to the right. We went through the door to the right. It opened into a large, dark, smoky room, the sort of backroom that featured in those Martin Scorsese films, such as Goodfellas or Casino - all that was missing was the playing cards.

'Sali, this is Mickey,' said Lisa.

Sali stood up and shook my hand. It was not the kind of welcome I had expected, still it was early evening and I noticed that, apart from Lisa, there were no other females in the room.

'Mickey, we meet at last, sit down… you hungry, do you like Chinese food? I hope so because that's all you'll fucking get here.' His words elicited smiles on the faces of what I assumed were his fellow gang members, who were sitting on either side of him. My first impression of Sali was not what I expected. I thought he would have a bit more about him, tough or scary looking perhaps, but no, he just looked like a normal guy. I suppose that's a good thing, the last thing you want to do when you're the boss of a multi-million-pound drug gang is to stand out from the rest. At his request I sat down opposite him. Lisa left the room. Sali picked up a bottle. I wondered if he was going to lob it at me.

'Drink?' he asked, holding up the bottle.

'Yes. I'll have water please.' I wanted to keep a clear head.

'Surely you want something stronger than that. Try some of this, it's a traditional Albanian whiskey.' He filled my glass to the brim.

I realised it was a test, so I took a sip and instantly regretted it when I started to choke a little.

'Fucking hell, you've only just met me and you're trying to kill me already,' I said, trying to regain my breath. My remark raised a laugh in the room and it sort of broke the ice.

'Too strong?' Sali asked, still laughing.

'Just a little,' I replied.

'I've heard a lot about you, Mickey.'

'All good I hope,' I said, still coughing.

'My friends in Spain speak highly of you, even some of my enemies.'

'Enemies?'

'I'm talking about Colin, the Colin who tried to screw me over but failed - because you my friend stopped him and for that he murdered your woman.'

Hearing Sali talking about the reason for Chrissie's death choked me up but I couldn't show any weakness in front of this man. The memory of her lying in the street in a body bag would haunt me for the rest of my life. All I felt at that moment was anger, but I had to put on my poker face. I think he realised that he had touched on a raw nerve because he didn't wait for a reply from me.

'I've heard a lot about you, Mickey, from getting injured in Afghanistan, losing your brother - and all that business with AK and his brothers. Lisa said you needed a job.'

This was news to me, I thought Sali was the one who wanted me. I didn't say anything, I just listened.

'I like what I hear about you Mickey. But I need more information.'

'What do you want, references, a CV?' There were a few nervous moments when I reached into my pocket and took out Peanut's mobile phone.

'It's ok, it's only a phone. I took it from Colin's brother Peanut,' I said.

I displayed the grizzly pictures of Peanut's holiday snaps to Sali.

'He was going to be my reference, but unfortunately he and his friend couldn't make it.'

Sali smiled. 'So, it was you who killed them. I hated them both.'

I went on to explain how they met their fate, over another glass of his Albanian aviation fuel

'I just want you to know Mickey we are not your typical Albanian street crew gang of drug dealers who are all over social media, showing off our Ferraris, wads of fifty-pound notes, gold Rolex watches and dishing out violence to help enhance its reputation. We like to go about our business quietly. We have a strong inner discipline in our clan, punishment ensures fear and fear guarantees unconditional loyalty. As a rule, we never take anyone in from the outside.'

I stood up. 'That's ok, I understand, I take it that it's time for me to leave,' I said.

'Sit down Mickey.'

There was an uncomfortable calm in the room. I looked straight at Sali's face but it did not give anything away, I felt like a losing gladiator in the middle of the arena waiting for Caesar to make the decision whether I was to live or die.

'But you are an exception. I know what you're capable of, but can you carry out my orders without hesitation? More importantly, can I trust you?'

'I trusted the army, but they abandoned me, I trusted AK and he nearly killed me, I trusted Colin and he murdered my woman. So, my question is, can I trust you Sali? I know that if you decide not to take me into your organization, you will, without doubt, kill me, or at least try to. All I'm saying is this - I've lost everything through trusting people, so to be honest, I don't give a shit if you trust me or not.'

'You've got some balls talking to me like that,' Sali answered.

He did not look happy about my statement. There was a long pause while he deliberated.

'We Albanians are known in criminal circles for being sophisticated, professional and for doing what we promise. We always deliver. We have an Albanian code called '*besa*' it means 'To keep the promise' but we also have an ancestral code called 'Kanun', the right to take revenge, blood must pay with blood.'

He then proffered his hand for me to shake.

'Welcome to our gang.'

I had been accepted against all the odds. It had been a gamble speaking to him as I had but it had paid dividends.

'Just one more thing,' he said, releasing my hand.

'And what's that?'

'Don't punch any more of my men in the throat. He was watching your back, making sure you were not being followed by anyone else.'

Ten minutes later we were all sitting in the restaurant, joined by Lisa and a few other women. I was welcomed with open arms and there was no more talk about business, it just felt like an enjoyable evening out with new friends. Eventually, once the evening was nearing its end, Sali pulled me to one side.

'Can I ask you one thing Mickey, why didn't you take your revenge on Colin, I don't understand?'

I was well on my way to being shit-faced, but I tried to answer him the best I could.

'I didn't know it was him that started the fire until I found the messages on Peanut's phone, then Lisa contacted me and told me what happened.'

'How did she find you?'

'Through an ex business partner - anymore questions?'

'No. No more questions Mickey. Listen, I might have a job for you in a few days, are you up for it?'

'I'm up for it, that's what I'm here for. What sort of job?'

'I'll tell you soon, when you haven't had too much to drink, in the meantime, just chill out in the flat, you should have everything you need in there.'

'Why, aren't I allowed out?'

'No, too risky. You are a wanted man. I only want you out when I need you. I'll be in touch.'

There was a car waiting for me outside the restaurant, Sali patted me on the back and I said my goodbyes to Lisa and my new partners in crime before getting in the car and leaving.

Back at the flat, I showered and went to bed, my mind was working overtime, I was asking myself question after question, going through the whole night from start to finish. Did I pull it off? If I had failed, I would be dead by now surely, shit, he will have keys to the flat. I sprang out of bed and looked out onto a deserted street, there was no one around, just the odd taxi. I decided to drag the dining table up against the door. At least if they did come tonight, I would hear them trying to get in. What am I doing? I must be fucking paranoid, I thought to myself, no, just watching my back. And just for good measure I placed a knife under my pillow. Providing I didn't have any of those fucked up dreams and no unwelcome guests, I would be alright.

Chapter 10

The next morning the sounds coming up from the busy road below woke me. My head was banging from the alcohol that I'd drunk at the restaurant, all I wanted to do was go back to sleep, but my bladder had other ideas. I headed for the bathroom to relieve myself and check the bathroom cabinet for paracetamol. Having found a box of paracetamol, I left the bathroom and walked to the kitchen to get a glass of water. On my way to the kitchen I noticed the dining table was back in its place in the living room. I quickly filled a glass with water and headed back to the bedroom. I checked under the pillow; the knife was gone. Shit, when did that dream start? I was totally confused, I put it down to being shit-faced. Yes, I was drunk.

I did nothing for the next two days, apart from pig out on large kebabs from the takeaway two doors down. I also purchased two bolt locks for the front door from the hardware shop, it was a bit of insurance. I wanted to ensure that the apartment was as secure as possible, especially after that dream, maybe it was a warning of things to come.

By day four I was starting to get really bored, I felt like just pissing off. I wondered when Sali would contact me. I needed to contact Bryant and give him an update. I waited until 7pm and took a walk to the friendly kebab shop and after promising I would order another large kebab and chips, they let me use their phone.

The sound of the phone ringing at the other end seemed to go on for ages, I was beginning to get impatient. 'Come on, answer the bloody phone for fuck's sake,' I muttered under my breath. I was just about to give up when the call was answered.

'Hi, you are through to DS Bryant…I'm not available to take your call, please leave a message after the tone.'

Well, that filled me with confidence. I hope I never need his help in a hurry.

'It's Mickey. All good so far. I have nothing for you yet. Oh, and next time I call, it would be nice to talk to someone and not a fucking answer phone.'

At 10am the next morning I heard a key being turned in the apartment door, who the hell was that trying to get in, unannounced. I was glad I had fitted the bolt locks. There was a gentle knock on the door. Whoever it was they had obviously realised that having a key did not give them automatic entrance to the apartment!

'Who is it?' I called out.

'It's me Mickey, let me in.'

I opened the door to Lisa and who I guessed must be her permanent bodyguard. I had seen him before at the train station. He looked a nasty piece of work.

'I've come to drop you some food off and give you a message from Sali. Well are you going to let me in?'

I stood to one side to let her in, she turned to her friend. 'It's ok Filip. You can wait for me in the car.'

He did not move a muscle, he just stared at us both.

'Filip, it's ok, I said go and wait in the car,' Lisa said more forcefully.

'How long?' he asked.

'I'll be ten minutes. I need to give this information to Mickey. It'll be ok, or do I have to phone Sali?'

At the mention of Sali's name Filip conceded defeat and started walking towards the car. I let Lisa into the apartment and closed the door.

'He's a bit possessive, isn't he?'

'Tell me about it, too bloody possessive. I'm sure he's undressing me every time he stares at me.'

'Why don't you tell Sali that he makes you feel uncomfortable?'

'Sali would kill him. He's ok, he just gives me the creeps. I haven't got much time, I've spoken to Bryant, he's up to date on everything.'

'I'm glad you got to speak to him, all I got was an answerphone.'

'You need to get ready, Sali wants to see you,' Lisa informed me.

'Why, what about?'

'I don't know, he never tells me anything, but I'm sure he's got a little job for you. By the way, he likes you, he told me that last night.'

'What about you, what are you doing?'

'I'm off up to Nottingham to see my mother, she's not well, it's just a day trip, I'll be back later tonight. I'm catching the train after I've dropped you off.'

'Is your friend going with you?'

'Who Filip?' 'No, he's giving him the day off. Sali is letting me go on my own. He can be ok sometimes. Just never cross him, he is pure evil, Mickey, I have seen it up close. Right, come on, we better get going.'

I locked up the flat and followed her to the waiting car. I got in the front with Filip. Lisa, looking very much like the lady of the manor, sat in the back. Nobody spoke but she was right about Filip. I noticed during most of the journey that he couldn't keep his eyes off her, constantly peering at her through the rear-view mirror. I felt like saying something but thought it wise not to. It was not long before we arrived at the restaurant, the one where I had met Sali for the first time.

'Time to get out, Mickey, I've got a train to catch. I'll see you soon,' Lisa said.

'Have a good journey,' I called back as I got out of the car.

I stood outside the restaurant for a few minutes to gather my thoughts. I was not sure if the summons from Sali was a friendly gesture or my death warrant. I heaved a sigh and entered the building Moments later I was sitting in front of Sali. At this meeting he was very business like, he sat behind a stylish desk with one of his clan never far away.

'Ready to do some business Mickey?' he asked.

'I thought you'd never ask. Sitting in that flat was driving me crazy. What have you got for me?'

'I am giving you Colin's old job, Mickey. I want you to do a bit of couriering for me. I'm giving you a hire car, inside the car, hidden under the back seat, is three 1kg blocks of compressed cocaine, each worth forty thousand pounds. I want you to drop off each block and collect the money. All the drops are in the Midlands area - Leicester, Burton and Nottingham.'

Sali went on for the next half hour telling me the who, when, where and what - in meticulous detail. I had to admire how organized he was.

'Did you understand all that?' he asked.

'Shouldn't be a problem. All these people I'll be dropping the gear off to, will they be ok dealing with someone new?'

'They know what car you'll be driving. I have given them your description and all your drops will be at church graveyards. To make sure you look the part we've put three sets of flowers in the car for you to carry.'

'Are you serious!' I started to chuckle.

'Mickey, it's the finer details that count. Don't worry, you'll be OK.'

'When do I leave?'

'The car will be ready in ten minutes. Oh, and on the way back you'll be picking up Lisa, she's visiting her sick mother.'

'I'd rather not Sali, I still haven't forgiven her for what happened in Spain.'

'Mickey, I assure you she had no part in that.' He started to smile. 'And I'm telling you to pick her up, you don't have to speak to her and for Christ sake don't tell her there's one hundred and twenty thousand pounds under her seat, she'll be straight down Oxford street to spend it all.'

'Do I get a phone, just in case?'

'In case of what? No phones, no weapons, we don't do that, the people who we deal with know that we don't fuck about.'

One hour later and I was driving up the M1 in a battered grey Vauxhall Astra with three 1kg blocks of compressed cocaine under the back seat and three bunches of wilting flowers. I wondered what I had got myself into. I pulled over at the services, making sure I was not being followed, but to be honest, I don't think he would have let me come this far without trusting me. I grabbed a coffee and reported into Bryant, giving him the full details of today's activities. He assured me there would not be any stings today, just surveillance and the gathering of evidence. Two hours later I arrived on the outskirts of Leicester. Using my built-in satnav, I found my way to the first graveyard, parked up nearby and grabbed the block of cocaine in its carrier bag - and a bunch of flowers! I was sure Sali was having a laugh. I took my time walking to the graveyard, my eyes constantly scanning the area. I walked through the gates and headed down the path as I had been instructed to. I stopped at a grave and placed the flowers on it, then stood as though in silent prayer. It was not long before I was approached by a couple, who were pushing a baby buggy.

'Mickey isn't it?' the male asked.

'Yes.'

'Nice to meet you,' he said, smiling.

We exchanged carrier bags and stood together at the graveside for a moment before parting company. He said 'Cheers' and they went on their way. Back in the car I thought how easy was that, nothing to it really and the next two drops were just as easy. I knew my next job would be a lot more difficult, taking Lisa back down to London. I would have to put up with her all the way down the M1. I picked her up from her mother's house around half past five. I expected non-stop chatter from her, but she was unusually quiet for the first part of the journey, which was a nice surprise. I broke the silence.

'How's your mum?'

'She's fine, thanks. How's your day been, what have you been up to?'

'Oh, you know…just couriering kilos of cocaine around the Midlands that's all, as you do.'

'Did you tell Bryant?'

'Yes, I did, but I don't think he was that interested. I didn't spot one of their surveillance teams. Either they were not there, or they were fucking good at the job.'

'Really?'

'I can't believe where I've ended up. One minute I am sunning it up in Spain, the next minute I am digging holes on a Scarborough beach and now I'm a courier for an Albanian drug gang. We don't have to do this shit,' I said.

'Yes, we do. It's for our freedom, Mickey.'

'So they say, but they missed out the bit where we could get killed. What the fuck are we doing, why are we putting ourselves through this shit? Do you know how much is under the car seat?'

'How much?'

'One hundred and twenty thousand pounds, we could just disappear right now, take the money and live like kings…for a while anyway. What do you reckon?'

'Hold on a minute, have you been laying flowers in graveyards by any chance?' she asked, laughing.

'Yes. I thought you didn't know what I was doing and why are you laughing?'

'There isn't any money under the seat, it's just bundles of paper, Mickey.'

'I don't believe you.'

We stopped at Leicester Forest services on the way to London. I got out of the car and asked Lisa to do the same, so that I could lift the back seat and examine one of the packages. I ripped it open to confirm what she had said. She was right, it was a few, fake, fifty-pound notes, which wouldn't have fooled anybody. They were cleverly layered with newspaper and wrapped in brown paper; I couldn't believe it.

'Sali is not going to be happy when he sees that you've opened that, looks like you've been had.'

I was confused. Why would he send me on a wild goose chase? It didn't make sense.'

'Relax, Mickey, he was testing you. What you gave those customers was just bags of flour. He did the same thing to Colin on his first job.'

I didn't know whether to laugh or cry, but I knew I would have to rewrap the package I had torn open. I stood there and shook my head in disbelief. I felt like a right dick-head, it reminded me of being back in the army, some of the pranks were legendary.

'Come on, I'll buy you a cappuccino, you multi-million pound cocaine courier you,' said Lisa, laughing.

'I can't believe I fell for that one.'

'No wonder Sali didn't want you to drop me off or tell me what you'd be doing. Anyway, look on the bright side, if there is one, you've passed his test with flying colours.'

'How did you work that out?'

'You didn't piss off with all his money and his drugs, thinking you were loaded.'

'Well the thought did cross my mind didn't it.'

'Or bottle it. What if you were being watched by the police, following your update to Bryant, if they had pounced that would have been funny. All you have to do now is go back and act dumb, let Sali have his moment.'

'That is if we make it back, look at the weather, there's a storm closing in.' As I spoke, large flakes of snow began to fall.

We hurried into the service station and while Lisa went to order some coffees and something to eat, I went to buy some brown paper and tape, to wrap the package up. Sitting in the restaurant, we watched as the falling snow thickened and turned into a blizzard. That night the whole of the Midlands was gridlocked and all major routes south were closed, due to the storm. Lisa phoned Sali and told him that we would not be making it back that night and we were heading for the nearest hotel.

'So, what did he say?' I said, driving slowly in the heavy snow.

'Surprisingly, he was ok with it, well what can he say he only has to look at the weather forecast. He probably sees it as another trust test.'

'What do you mean?' I asked.

Lisa smiled and looked out of the window. We found a small hotel just off the motorway and booked into separate rooms. I spent my time re-wrapping the opened package before taking a shower and having a short nap. We met in the bar later that evening and Lisa was looking stunning as usual.

'Drink?' she asked.

'I'll get it,' I said.

'Nonsense, Sali is paying,' she replied, waving a credit card.

'Well, in that case, I'll have a double whiskey with ice.'

We picked up our drinks and sat down in the corner of the bar.

'I can't believe how dumb I've been,' I said, referring to the job I had been given.

'Don't worry about it, you're not the first or the last to fall for it. Anyway, you make a good flour salesman, remind me how much you made today.'

'Very fucking funny,' I replied, we both laughed. 'Changing the subject, how is your mum?'

'She's very poorly, she has dementia. I need to be seeing her more often, the poor thing, this is another reason why I want this over with, Mickey. I've had enough of this life.' She looked so sad as she spoke.

We sat quietly for a few minutes; I think we both had regrets about the circumstances that had brought us to the situation we were now in. I sat staring into my glass, wondering if I would still be alive at the end of it. I glanced up and caught Lisa staring intently at my neck.

'That's a nice locket, who's in it, your mother?'

'No, Chrissie and my son Matthew.' I opened it up to show her.

'That's beautiful.'

'I'll never take it off ever.'

'I get that, Mickey. I know how much you loved her, I could tell when I met her, she was a lovely woman. You do believe me when I say I had nothing to do with what happened over there don't you?'

As she spoke, her eyes brimmed with tears, so she was human after all.

'Yes, I do, but can we not talk about it.'

'I'm sorry.'

She looked relieved when I said I believed her. We didn't talk for a while. I couldn't think of anything to say. Talking about Chrissie had choked me up. After a late dinner and a few drinks, we were more relaxed and we both became a little more friendly with each other. I was starting to enjoy her company and warm to her more. I could now see what AK, Colin and now Sali saw in her, as well as her good looks and sense of humour, she seemed to have the power to draw you in.

'Can I ask you a question, Mickey, if that had been real money, would you have done a runner?'

'Too right.'

'And would you have taken me with you?'

'Would you have come?'

'Maybe, but it wouldn't solve our problem. Don't you want a normal life, Mickey?'

'Yes, but I don't trust the Police, do you? We'll still end up doing time eventually.'

'But it might only be a few months,' Lisa said.

'For you maybe, it's only a matter of time before they find out who killed Peanut and Josh, I'm sure. What sentence do they give for murder, twenty years, life? They might knock a few years off if we can pull this off, but I'd be in my late fifties when I walk free. So yes, I would do a fucking runner alright. So how did a pretty girl like you get mixed up in all this, Lisa, why do you always end up with the bad boy? AK, Colin and now Sali.'

She paused before she spoke, as though what she was about to say caused her immense pain.

'When I was about thirteen, I got bullied a lot at school. I tried to put on a front, but I just ended up in lots of fights. I decided I wanted to get off with a bad boy, no one could touch me then...and it worked. I met a lad of fifteen, he had a bit of a reputation as a dealer, he always had money and he was nice to me, I could trust him, look up to him. Suddenly my life had changed, overtaken by the gang he ran, no one could touch me because I had friends who would have my back. I left school at sixteen and we moved into a flat together. Before long, he was asking me to do this and that, weighing out portions of drugs and wrapping them in cling film. Soon, I was dropping off packages, which included ferrying his gun. Nobody suspected me, the pretty, innocent looking girl. It never crossed my mind that anything could happen to me. I was told that if I got caught with the gun I just had to keep on saying 'No comment, no comment.' I was lucky I never got caught. As time went on, I was drawn deeper into gang life. Did I love him?

Probably not. I just believed I did and then one day it all changed...the day I told him I was pregnant. He told me to get rid of it - we had an argument and then he hit me for the first time. By that time, he had become AK, someone that nobody fucked with.'

'That's a pretty sad story, so what about Sali, do you have any feelings for him?'

'No, not now I've seen the other side of him, he's evil, worse than AK or Colin.'

'Do you know how he ended up where he is now?'

'Not really, all I know is that he arrived here in the late nineties', about the time of the Kosovan War. He got into the country by claiming to be Kosovan and requesting asylum. His brother, and his inner circle, all arrived at the same time.'

What she said made sense. I had heard similar stories over the years of gangs using the asylum laws to move their operations to more lucrative countries.

'I know how we can get hold a lot of money and it's money that isn't on the Police radar. Mickey, we can just slip away.' I could hear the desperation in her voice.

'How?'

Lisa explained her plan and I listened for the next half hour. It was a good plan, probably too good to be true.

'That sounds too easy.'

'Because it is easy, Mickey. We need to know when the next drug shipment is coming, just to keep the Police happy, then everyone is a winner.'

'Apart from Sali and his gang.'

'Correct.'

'Tuesday morning, that's when the drugs come in.'

'What, how do you know, has Sali told you?'

'I just know that's all, long story. But I need to confirm it, things change. The only person to know for sure is Sali. Can't you work your magic on him?'

'You don't know Sali do you? It's like getting blood out of a stone. You will know when it is when he is ready to tell you and not before. He is very clever, not easily fooled, that's why he has been in the game a long time. So, what do you think?'

'It could work, but we'll need a lot of luck. Does he ever get jealous?'

'Jealous, what about?'

'Aren't you worried about what Sali will say about us spending the night together?'

'But I'm not spending the night with you am I.'

'You know what I mean.'

'No, I don't. Shall we give him a reason to be worried, I'm up for it if you are,' she said, looking straight at me.

Well, there was an offer I couldn't refuse. But that night I did refuse. I'm sure there will be a time for that, after all, I have needs, but Chrissie was still very fresh in my memory. I walked her to her bedroom door, gave her a hug and said Goodnight.

'Goodnight Mickey and if you change your mind, just knock.'

'Do you really want another bad boy?'

'You're not a bad boy, Mickey, far from it, a bit crazy, but not a bad boy.'

Chapter 11

The following morning the sky was bright and clear, not a flake of snow was falling. The only evidence of the previous night's blizzard were the mounds of snow that had been pushed to the side of the paths around the hotel. I hurriedly got showered and dressed and went to wake up Lisa, we needed to get back on the road as soon as possible. Lisa answered the door almost immediately, she was wearing one of the thick, white, towelling robes, supplied by the hotel. She opened the door wider to let me enter the room.

'I won't be long, I've just got to brush my teeth,' she said, disappearing into the bathroom.

I could hear water running in her bathroom. I glanced around the room, her clothes were placed in a neat pile on the bed, which she had taken the time to tidy up. I hoped she wouldn't take too long as I wanted to grab a quick bite to eat before we left. I heard the bathroom door open and turned to face it. Lisa was framed in the doorway, stark naked, my body began to respond, which she noticed. She walked over to me and stroked the bulge in my trousers. Lifting her head, she kissed me gently on the lips.

'When this is over you can explore every inch of my body and I'm looking forward to that day,' she said, giving my lower lip a playful nip with her teeth.

It took all my reserves not to throw her on the bed and screw her. She knew how to turn a guy on. Before I knew it, she was on her knees and taking my throbbing cock in her mouth. I hadn't felt her undo my flies. I couldn't pull away, I was enjoying it too much. As I began ejaculating, I thought she would pull away, but she didn't. It took ages to bring my ragged breathing under control. I felt guilty that I had enjoyed it so much. Lisa stood up and gave me another kiss, this time more passionately. I knew I had to stop this before we ended up in bed, so I placed my hands on her shoulders and gently pushed her away.

'Didn't you like it?' she asked, looking hurt.

'Too much, that's the problem,' I replied. 'If we let it go any further don't you think Sali will notice.'

'I hadn't thought about him. When all this shit is over, Mickey, I want you to make love to me all day and night.' She moved away from me, looking sad and started to get dressed.

We ate a quick breakfast in the hotel restaurant, then we were back on the road. The problem being, so was everyone else. So many people must have had the same idea of sheltering from the bad weather.

'Hopefully, all this will be over in a few days and Sali's gang will be no more,' I said, hoping to cheer her up.

'It just opens up opportunities for more gangsters to swoop in, all the coppers do is get rid of the competition,' Lisa replied.

'That plan you talked about last night, you still up for it?' I asked.

'What, run off into the sunset with you, Mickey? Yes, now more than ever.' Lisa rubbed her hand on my leg and smiled. 'We just need a few things to go our way that's all.'

'Fuck it, let's do it,' I said.

After spending most of the day on the M1 and going over and over her plan, we made it back to London. Lisa asked me to drop her off at home, not at the restaurant. I was a bit dubious about doing that, I didn't know how my new boss would react.

'Will that be ok? I thought Sali was a little bit secretive about where he lives.'

'I live there too you know and it's in my name, plus he won't be there, he'll be at the restaurant waiting for you to return. Just tell him you dropped me off in the village. Say I wanted to freshen up for him before he gets home.'

Suddenly I was a little jealous and wished I had taken her up on her offer the previous night and earlier this morning.

Following her instructions, we soon arrived on her street. I don't think there was one property worth less than three million pounds! I planned to give Lisa a goodnight kiss, but something had caught her attention.

'Hold on - carry on driving - don't stop - something's not right.'

I drove a short distance and pulled over further down the road. I hadn't noticed anything strange or out of place on the street, but Lisa obviously had.

'What is it, what's wrong?' I asked.

'The light was on and the curtains are open. If Sali is home that's something he would never do,' she answered.

We got out of the car and walked back down the road towards the house. As we approached, I noticed a car suddenly speeding off, a car I had seen somewhere before.

'Stay here,' I said.

156

As I walked up the steps to Sali's house I noticed the front door was half open. I entered the house, moving down the corridor quietly. Although the sound was slightly muffled by music being played, I could hear someone getting a right kicking.

'Give me the fucking code!' I heard someone shout.

The door leading to the dining room was slightly open. All I could see was a large male figure, with his back to me, he was dressed in black, wearing a balaclava and holding a gun in his bandaged right hand. In front of him, lying on the floor was Sali, his voice barely legible. The gun was now pointing at Sali's head.

'I'll ask you one more time, what is the code? Tell me the fucking code or I will shoot you in the fucking head, you cunt.'

After a few more kicks to his back and rib cage, Sali gave his safe number. His voice was faint but I memorized every number and letter that he uttered, that code would come in useful if Lisa's plan became a reality.

'This better be right,' Sali's tormentor growled.

The intruder walked over to the safe and started to tap in the code, by this time I had sneaked into the room and was standing right behind him. The music he had put on to muffle Sali's cries for help had prevented him from hearing my approach. He tapped in the last digits before he realised I was there, but by then it was too late, my hammer came crashing down on his head and then again for good measure. The intruder fell to the ground, he was now laying on his back, his head lying in a pool of his own blood, he was in a semi-conscious state when I sat on him and proceeded to pull off his balaclava.

His next words were 'fuck me, not you and your hammer again,' then he passed out just as I was about to strike him again.

Lisa entered the room and began to attend to Sali, who had taken a bit of a kicking. I stood up and watched the pool of blood, behind the intruder's head, as it spread.

'Have you killed him?' Lisa asked, as she continued helping Sali.

'Nah, he'll be ok'

With Lisa's help, Sali was now on his feet. His left eye was beginning to swell and his lower lip was split open, he bent slightly forward, obviously the kicking he had taken to his back and ribs was causing him some pain.

'Are you ok darling? Sit down,' Lisa said, trying to comfort him.

'I'm fine,' he said, lowering himself onto a chair. 'So, I bet this is all your ex boyfriend's doing. Colin is going to fucking pay for this,' Sali replied.

Just then, Erald, Sali's right hand man, turned up. He glanced around the room looking confused.

'What's happening - who's he?' he asked, pointing at Merv.

'I think it's one of Colin's men,' Sali replied.

'Where were you? You're supposed to be looking after Sali,' Lisa said.

'I dropped him off ten minutes ago. I just went to get a pizza.'

'Didn't you see them? You must have been followed,' Lisa persisted.

'Ok, can we stop the blame game, we need to get rid of this body,' Sali interjected.

'But he's not dead,' I said.

'Do you want me to strangle him?' Erald asked.

'Mickey, take him out somewhere in the car and see what information you can get out of him, then shoot him. Use his own gun. Sali instructed me.

I picked up the gun and put it in my waistband.

'I can do that,' said Erald.

'I'm asking Mickey to do it, you can go with him, just get this fucking scum-bag out of my sight.'

Erald's face was a picture; you could tell he didn't like Sali's decision. Together we lifted Merv off the blood-soaked floor. He was starting to come around and by the time we got him to Erald's car he was awake. We laid him in the back seat and I got in alongside him.

'So where are we going?' I asked.

'It's ok, leave it to me, I know just the place,' Erald replied.

He drove us to a wooded area next to a golf course, the nearest houses were about half a mile away. By the time we got there Merv was sitting up. I held the gun to his head, I think he soon realised the danger he was in, judging by how much he was trembling.

'Please don't shoot me, my girlfriend is about to have a baby, we're going to get married at Christmas. I wasn't going to kill him, Colin told me to do the robbery and rough him up a bit,' he pleaded, as tears ran down his face.

It looked like I wouldn't have to try hard to get any information out of him, he was squealing like a pig. I felt sorry for him in a way, he was just a kid who'd been dragged into someone else's fight.

'I love it when they beg for their lives, it just makes me want to shut them up even more. You were a big hard gangster an hour ago. Now look at you. You pathetic piece of shit!' Erald said.

We drove about one hundred metres down a short track and pulled up, we dragged him out of the car and lead him into the wood, at gun point. All the time he was praying for his life. We soon arrived at a small clearing.

'Here will do,' Erald said. 'Just shoot the bastard, I want to get back, its freezing.'

'Get down on your knees,' I instructed Merv.

He dropped to his knees, facing away from me, as I put the gun to his head he began to sob.

'Please don't kill me, I'll do anything, tell you anything,' he pleaded.

'Shut him up, put him out of his misery.' I could tell from Erald's attitude that he found the whole situation boring. He was beginning to piss me off.

'You heard what Sali said, I need to ask him some questions.'

'He's out of bargaining chips, he's already told us what we need to know, in the car,' Erald replied.

I realised I couldn't kill this kid, what has he done? He was no older than twenty and was no Peanut, he just got mixed up with some bad people. He deserved a second chance.

'Well, what are you waiting for Mickey?' Erald was growing impatient.

I froze, I couldn't pull the trigger, it didn't seem right or fair to end this kid's life for following orders. I didn't want to be his executioner.

'I thought so, you come down here with this big reputation, you might have fooled Sali but you ain't fooling me. Pull it, pull the fucking trigger or I'll cut his fucking head off!' raged Erald, brandishing a knife.

Then I heard a voice in my head. It was my brother. 'Shoot him Mickey, he's a cunt… shoot him.'

That was all I needed to hear, I pointed the gun at Erald's head and pulled the trigger. The gun failed to fire. I tried again, nothing! Before I knew it, Erald had rushed me with his knife. He stabbed me in the arm before I managed to kick it out of his hand, but in doing so I slipped backwards. Now I was at his mercy, he was on top of me with his hands around my throat. Erald was a strong man and must have weighed around twenty stones. I looked straight in his eyes and could see he was an angry man. His grip got tighter and tighter and I started to lose consciousness. Then the pressure stopped and his hands fell away. I started to recover my senses, as this giant of a bloke lay limp on top of me. I heaved him to one side and sat up. My face felt sticky with blood.

'I've killed him, Mickey, I've killed him.'

Lying alongside me was the lifeless body of Erald, with his throat sliced clean open. Merv was around five metres away, curled up next to a tree, rocking backwards and forwards with the bloodied knife in his hand.

'You're not going to kill me are you, Mickey?' he asked looking fearful.

I knelt in front of him and took the knife from his hand.
The last thing I needed right now was for him to turn
psycho on me.

'No mate. Don't worry, you're going home, but we've got
work to do first.'

We carried Erald's body to one of the golf course bunkers
at the edge of the wood, it was easier and quicker to dig
Erald's grave in the sand. We buried him two feet down.
Ten minutes later we sat in the car in silence. I could not
believe what had just happened. One minute I was hitting
this guy in the head with a hammer to within an inch of his
life, now we were partners in crime. Merv was still
shaking, which didn't surprise me, this kid had just had the
worst few hours of his life. He reminded me of myself as a
young soldier on my first tour of Afghanistan.

'How's your head?' I asked.

'Hurts a bit, but I'll live,' he replied.

'Have you got enough money to get back to Derby?'

'No.'

I handed him some money. 'Here, have this, I think there's
a few hundred pounds there. I'll drop you off near the
station, get yourself back up to Derby, look after your
girlfriend and baby and tell Colin you've quit. Oh, and I
suggest you pay a visit to the toilets, you need to clean
yourself up a bit before buying your train ticket. I never
want to see or hear about you again. I mean it.'

'Don't worry, you won't.'

I dropped him off at the underground station, luckily there
were not many people around as he got out of the car and
said goodbye. I was hoping he would take my advice, but I

remember thinking that I wouldn't hold my breath. My thoughts quickly turned to Sali and Lisa, how the hell am I going to explain what has just happened, his right-hand man had just been killed.

I arrived back at Sali's and I sat outside in the car, I still did not have a clue what to say, then it just came to me. Lisa saw me on the CCTV and came down the steps to greet me. I got out of the car.

'Mickey, what happened, you're covered in blood. Look at you, your face is covered in it.'

'Lisa, Erald's dead, I had to kill him. Whatever I tell Sali, just agree with me.'

I walked into the house wondering what kind of reception I would get from Sali. I didn't have to wait long to get my answer.

'What the fuck has happened Mickey, where's Erald?'

'You were set up, Sali,' I replied. 'We went to the golf course and we carried the kid into the woods. I told him to kneel and pointed the gun at his fucking head. I was just going to shoot the scumbag when Erald, fuck knows why, lunged at me for some reason and I dropped the gun. The next minute he was on top of me with his knife, trying to stab me.'

'What did I tell you, Sali, about that piece of shit, Erald, I never liked or trusted him,' said Lisa, interrupting me.

I continued with my story. 'When Erald was on top of me I asked him what the fuck he was doing.' Then he stabbed me in the arm. I kept asking him again and again why was he doing this. I was trying to fight him off for fucking ages then I started to get the better of him, so I took the knife off him and stabbed him in the neck. I had no fucking choice,

Sali, it was either him or me, I killed him. I made sure he was dead, that's for certain.'

'And the other one?'

'I think he was dead already. But I slit his throat for good measure. I can't understand it, why would Erald do that? Unless you ordered my killing, Sali?' I asked, with a straight face.

'No Mickey, why would I want you dead? I brought you in to take over from him, I saw it coming but I didn't think he would act so soon. I remember some of the men warning me that Erald wanted to take over and that he did not like the way I was running things. That piece of shit. It all makes sense, it was a set up, he wanted me dead and made it look like a robbery. Him and Colin were best mates when he was around. Dropping me off and then telling me he was off to get a pizza and leaving the door open, knowing those fuckers were waiting for me. He was hoping to come back and find me dead and I would have been had you two not turned up when you did.'

'There was no pizza in the car, Sali,' I told him.

'Where are the bodies?'

'Don't worry, no one will find them for a while. I buried them both deep in the bunker, near a clearing.'

'I think I know where you mean. That bastard was waiting for his moment, but he picked the wrong one. I owe you, Mickey. You and Lisa saved my life and for that I'll always be grateful.'

I stayed at Sali's place that night. After cleaning myself up, Lisa bandaged my arm while Sali was busy in the kitchen, talking on the phone, arranging to get rid of the hire car. He spoke in English and Albanian during the calls. Later, after eating, we all sat and drank until the early hours. I think we all needed a drink or two, especially me. That had to be the biggest load of bollocks I had ever gotten away with since I was in the army. Bullshit baffles brains, is what they used to say. I was sleeping on the sofa, but before Sali went to bed, he told me he had something big to tell me in the morning. I wondered what it was.

The next morning, we were all up, drinking coffee, last night's events were still in our minds. Then the conversation soon turned towards my couriering adventure around the Midlands. It was time for even more 'play acting', I was letting Sali have his moment. I laughed along with him when he explained it was a test of my loyalty, suddenly, Erald was confined to the history books.

'Now it is time to get serious, Mickey, after the fun and games of last night, I know that I can trust you one hundred percent, you are a good man, Mickey, a loyal man. That is exactly what I need right now, so today I am going to make you my right-hand man, what do you say?'

Lisa sat quietly listening to our conversation.

'I don't know what to say, Sali, what about the other gang members?'

'You don't have to say anything, none of my gang are suited for the job, apart from one and he's now on the golf course. Anyway, they all respect me and will do as they are told, they will respect you too. So, what do you say?'

'No more flour and flowers? This is not another wind up is it?'

'No more flour and flowers, Mickey, from now on it's the real thing.'

'I'm honoured, Sali.' I reached forward to shake his hand. What he told me next was music to my ears.

'I have to fly out to Marbella tonight. I have an important meeting. I have business matters to sort out. So, I need you to look after things for me while I am away. But your first job is an important one. Tomorrow they'll be a consignment coming in.'

'Consignment?'

'Cocaine, a lot of it.'

'How much is a lot?'

'Five hundred Kilos.'

Sali went on to give me all the details. He explained how they used legitimate trucking and logistics enterprises as cover to smuggle large quantities of cocaine, cannabis, amphetamines and people into Britain from the Netherlands and Spain...but I knew most of that already. The drop was going to happen tomorrow, Tuesday, and yes, you guessed it, the destination was the old deserted abattoir. A container lorry, full of tomatoes, will arrive at 11am, the cocaine will be hidden inside wooden pallets, the pallets were to be transferred into two, hired, three-ton vehicles and transported to one of Sali's two lockups in the city, his drug factories, where the cocaine will be extracted. I had no doubt that once the cocaine was removed from the pallets it would be contaminated with mixing agents, using hand blenders, mixers and accessories to adulterate the drugs, to increase the volume of the drug to be sold. After filling me in with more of the finer details, Sali stood up.

'I'll arrange for one of the guys to come and pick you up and take you to the restaurant at 7.30 am, the others will fill you in when you get there. I do not want you to take command on this job, Mickey, my brother, Bledor, will deal with it, the other guys know what to do, so just watch and learn. Right, I have a plane to catch.'

Filip arrived to take Sali to the airport, Lisa and I joined him in the car. The plan was to drop me off at my flat while Lisa saw Sali off. We both knew that Filip would be back to take up his duties of looking after Lisa. Wherever Lisa went, Filip went, but Lisa had other ideas.

'I think this is your stop, Mickey,' Sali said, as the car halted outside the electrical shop.

I wished Sali a good trip and said my goodbyes. I was now standing on the pavement outside my flat watching the car pull away, a smiling Lisa looked back at me from the rear window. Our exit plan was now in motion. After all that had happened, I could not believe that Sali had put that much faith in me. I needed to find a phone. I walked down the road to use the pay phone at the underground station.

This time I got through straight away. I spent a good thirty minutes filling DS Bryant in with all the details, I even told them about the restaurant, Sali's house and where the lockups were, but I had a feeling they knew about these places already. All they wanted to know was where and when…and now they knew. They now had twenty-four hours to plan their raid. After leaving the underground station I sat and waited in the flat for Lisa to contact me. It was a few hours later when I received the text.

Mickey are you ok?

I texted back.

Yes U?

My phone pinged again.

As I can be. This ape won't leave me alone. I'm in bed now. I have everything I need, well nearly everything. I just need the code.

I tapped in my reply.

SALI 447E3200

Lisa texted back.

I'll see you tomorrow morning at 7am, be ready Mickey. Tomorrow we'll be free.

I responded.

We will, be careful Lisa be seeing you very soon. missing you xxx

Lisa replied.

And you xxx

I didn't sleep much that night. I lay there worrying about Lisa, so far everything was going too smoothly for my liking.

Chapter 12

I got up at 5 am, made myself a coffee and sat waiting for Lisa to turn up. I wonder what they will think when they find the flat empty. Nothing I expect, they will go ahead with the pickup, someone has too, its five hundred kilos of cocaine, they will probably think I just bottled it. If everything goes to plan this morning it will all be over and I will be miles away, rich and free…well, sort of free. I checked my watch it was quarter to six, Lisa would be putting her plan into action by now. I heard a faint knock on my door, surely that's not Lisa already, it's too early I thought.

'Who is it?' I called out.

'Mickey, it's Bledor, Sali's brother, we have to leave early, there are road works on the M25. If we do not leave now, we'll be late for the drop off.'

What could I do, tell him I was ill and was calling in sick? I had to let him in, maybe I could do a runner at some stage, then contact Lisa to come and pick me up. What a fucking mess, I knew it was going too well, but little did I know things were about to get worse, a lot worse. I cautiously undid the two bolts and opened the door; receiving a greeting that I didn't expect. Everything went dark, I had been struck with something. I dropped to the floor.

When I woke up, I was slouched on one of the dining chairs in the centre of the living room, there were four gang members in the room with me. Was I having a bad dream? Was any of this real? I soon realized that this was no dream, it was real. I felt a sharp pain on the top of my head, probably caused by a blow from the baseball bat, that didn't belong to me, that lay on the coffee table. The silence in the room was unnerving, none of them spoke.

'What's going on? This is no way to treat a new member. I get it, this is some sort of initiation ceremony isn't it?' I said, even though I knew it was far from it.

They still refused speak, just stood staring at me like I was the latest exhibit in a museum. The cheeky bastards had made themselves drinks, which was evident by the number of mugs on the coffee table. The room stunk of cigarette smoke and the ashtray was overflowing with cigarette butts.

'I take it there are no hold ups on the M25 then?' I asked, hoping to get a response.

One of the gang members walked towards me, grabbed my hair and lifted my head to the light. I recognized him; he was the one that I'd throat punched a few days ago, out on the street near this flat. With the strong light in my eyes, I didn't see the punch coming, but I felt my nose break.

'Why are you doing this, what the fuck have I done to deserve this?' I asked them, still hoping for some response.

Still there was no answer. I was clueless about what was going on, they were obviously still interested in me or I would be dead by now. Did they know I was a police rat? If they did, I needed to brace myself for much worse treatment, some serious torture was coming my way. My wrists were tied behind my back but I still had the use of my legs, my only escape route was to make a dash for it by running straight at the window and crashing through the glass out onto the street below. I was deep in thought when I heard a familiar voice, it was Sali. What the fuck was he doing here? My thoughts turned to Lisa, did he know about our plan, was she alright?

'Mickey, how are the boys treating you? Badly, I hope. Are you listening to me, Mickey?'

I looked up, expecting to see him standing there, but he was not in the room. His brother held a mobile phone in front of my face. Sali grinned back at me from the screen.

'Mickey, I have to admit you nearly fooled me. But did you really think I would be that stupid. You made a grave mistake the other night my friend, for one thing, it was me that sent Erald for the pizza. It was me, Mickey, and you left the pizza in the car. I can even tell you what fucking flavour it was. But the biggest give-away was when my boys did a little fact checking, there was one body in bunker twelve and that was Erald. So, what happened to the fuckwit who tried to kill me? The fuckwit who obviously knew you by his comment, 'fuck me not you and your hammer again' is what he said. Now I would like to know what lies you are going to come up with to save your skin, but I'm guessing Colin is involved. Your little plan of worming your way into my organization failed, Mickey. I am sure my boys will find out the truth and then they will have their revenge for Erald's death. If you are not there when I get back, I won't lose any sleep over it. By the way, Mickey, the weather in Marbella is amazing.' He laughed as he ended the call.

I prepared myself for more punishment. The one good thing to come out of that conversation was the fact he didn't mention Lisa's name, hopefully she was safe and would get away from this life, that's if Bryant did his job well.

'We are running late, we need to hit the road. Tie him up good, we'll sort him out when we get back,' Bledor told his men, as he headed for the door.

Meanwhile at Sali's house, Lisa began to put her plan in action.

Lisa glanced at her alarm clock, 5.50 am, time to get up. She got out of bed and walked down the hallway, singing to herself as she headed towards the bathroom, wearing just her knickers. She wanted to make sure Filip was awake. Lisa wanted him to see her, she made sure he did by walking past the open door of the guest bedroom. She entered the bathroom and intentionally left the door slightly ajar. Filip did not need an invitation; he was quickly on his feet and outside the bathroom door. Sensing he was there; she slowly took off her knickers and climbed into the shower. She made a point of lathering her breasts with shower gel before continuing down her body to her crotch area.

Filip was instantly aroused by her display, he knew that if Sali found out what he was doing, he would be in big trouble, but it was worth it. He had been watching her for months and she knew it, he was certain of that.

Lisa climbed out of the shower and began to towel herself down before reaching for a jar of moisturizer and rubbing it into her body, paying particular attention to her breasts. She hoped her little show was having the desired effect. She lifted her head and glanced towards the door. Their eyes met.

'You naughty boy, have you been standing there the whole time? she asked in a husky voice.

'You knew I was there, you cock teasing bitch,' he replied, conscious of the bulge in his trousers.

Filip blocked the bathroom door with his body as Lisa tried to pass him. He eventually moved slightly to one side, so that she would have to brush past him.

'You know why I took a shower don't you? This is all for you Filip, I've seen the way you look at me all the time, practically undressing me. Well, here is your big chance, Sali will not be back for a few days. Do you want some fun? I know I do. I won't tell him if you won't,' she whispered in his ear breathlessly.

She slowly squeezed past an excited Filip, making sure her hand brushed the bulge in his trousers and walked back to her bedroom. Filip followed her, unable to believe that his long-held dream of screwing her was about to come true. He hesitated in the doorway, wondering if this was a kind of test, set up by Sali, everyone knew he constantly tested his gang members loyalty, but the primeval urge to have sex overrode his concerns and he entered the room.

'Well, come on, let me see what you've got,' urged Lisa, sensing his hesitation.

Filip started to undress; he could not believe his luck. Lisa walked towards the walk-in wardrobe, opened the doors and began searching through the racks of clothes.

'Let me see what I've got, what would you like me to wear, how about this?'

Lisa held up a sexy, black, faux leather, bondage-style lingerie set. With her eye on the time she quickly put it on and approached Filip, who was now lying naked on the bed. Lisa climbed onto the bed to join him. Before he knew it, she was sitting on his chest with her crotch close to his face. His hands rose to fondle her breasts, she pushed them away.

'Not so fast, we need to have some fun first. Every man's fantasy is to be handcuffed to the bed, Sali loves it.'

Filip is totally under her spell; he sees no reason why Lisa would not want him and so he doesn't resist. At that moment he would let her do whatever she wanted, his barriers were down, but his cock was most definitely up. Filip is a strong, powerful, overweight and ugly man, covered in body hair and always smelling of garlic. Lisa found him repulsive, that's why Sali gave him the job of looking after her, he knew there would be no way Lisa would go near him, until now! Filip is now at her disposal, spread-eagled on Sali's bed and there was no escape, the bed is made of solid oak and the handcuffs were the real thing. Filip still believed he was in for the time of his life; he certainly wasn't expecting what happened next. Lisa returned to the wardrobe and reappeared with a cane in her hand. She began striking Filip's naked body, much to his displeasure. He bit his lip to avoid crying out in pain.

'What's wrong Filip? I see your erection has disappeared, aren't I doing it for you, don't you fancy me anymore?' Lisa asked, laughing.

'Ok, that's enough, you've had your fucking fun you slut, let me go,' he replied, struggling to try and break free.

Lisa struck him again, even harder, this time across the face.

'I'm not putting up with that sort of language.'

She stopped striking him and climbed onto his chest to tape his mouth up with masking tape, to stop him shouting out. It was obvious he was not happy as he pulled at the handcuffs.

Lisa got off the bed and picked up her phone and started to take a few snaps of Filip spread-eagled on the bed.

'Sali is going to love these,' she said.

Looking at the clock on the bedside cabinet, she realized she was running late. Blowing Filip a kiss, she grabbed her clothes and headed to the bathroom to get dressed. Returning to the bedroom, she sat at the dressing table to put the finishing touches to her look. Looking in the mirror, to apply the final touches to her makeup, she could see that Filip was still trying his hardest to break away from his handcuffs. Checking her watch, she knew it was time to empty the safe. Walking downstairs to the dining room, she hoped Mickey's memory was good. She tapped in the code that he had given her and the safe was open. Standing back in amazement, she could not believe her eyes, all the time she had lived in the house with Sali she never knew for certain what was in the safe, but had guessed it would contain money. There was bundle after bundle of bank notes in large denominations, bags of cocaine, jewellery, even a few gold bars and a pistol. Lisa took everything, emptying it into two large grips. After taking photos of the empty safe, she put on her coat and walked back upstairs to the bedroom to say her goodbyes to Filip.

'Don't worry Filip, the Police will be along soon to rescue you, don't look so sad.'

Lisa shook a set of car keys in front of him, the ones she had retrieved from the living room.

'Oh, I need your car. You don't mind, do you?'

The drive to the apartment seemed to take forever, Lisa heaved a sigh of relief when she eventually arrived outside the apartment. She ran up the stairs and knocked on the door.

'Mickey, open the door!' she called out.

She stood waiting for him to open the door, but nothing happened, so she knocked even harder on the door. She was eager for them both to put some distance between them and London and the danger it held.

'Mickey, come on, open the door!!' she shouted.

The door was opened, but not by Mickey, it was one of Sali's gang members, which took her by surprise.

'What are you doing here?' she asked, as she walked into the apartment. 'Where's Mickey?'

She noticed a second gang member standing in the room. Both men looked at each other before the one who had opened the door replied.

'Mickey is not here.'

'Where is he then?' Lisa asked, feeling a sense of rising panic.

'He's gone with the others, Lisa, they had to leave early, heavy traffic on the M25.'

'Really?'

'Yes.'

'So why are you two here?'

'Bledor told us to stay here, there wasn't enough room for us.'

Lisa knew they were lying. Her suspicions were proved correct when she noticed something shining on the wooden floor, slightly hidden by one of the coffee table legs, it was Mickey's locket. She remembered what he had told her about never taking it off. She quickly focused her eyes on the gang members, hoping they had not seen her staring at the locket.

'Ok, I might as well go back home,' she said.

'Where is Filip?' asked the other gang member, taking her by surprise.

'Filip is not very well, he's got a fever so I left him in bed, he's even lost his voice. I came out to go to the chemist to pick up some medicine for him. I need to get back and look after him. Listen, when Mickey gets back, tell him to contact me. Oh, I just had a thought, I've got something in the car that was supposed to be for Mickey but as he's not here you two might as well have it. I won't be long,' replied Lisa, as she left the apartment, leaving the door slightly ajar.

The two men waited for Lisa to return, expecting some sort of treat. Lisa being Sali's girlfriend they would never have expected what happened next. Moments later, Lisa reappeared in the doorway, brandishing a semi-automatic pistol.

'Get down on the ground both of you!' Lisa ordered.

'Lisa, what are you doing?' one of the men asked, confused by her actions.

'Get down now!' she demanded.

The gang member who had earlier opened the door, lunged at her, but fell short as she stepped back and fired the pistol. Lisa was a lousy shot, but luckily for her, although not for him, she shot him in the bollocks. As he lay on the floor, groaning in agony, she trained her pistol at the other gang member.

'Don't shoot, Lisa, don't shoot, please,' he begged, unnerved by the cries of agony from his friend.

Lisa stooped down and picked up the locket and shoved it in his face.

'Where is he?' she asked.

'He's in the bath,' he replied shakily, his eyes fully trained on the pistol.

Lisa fired another shot, this time it was accidental. She must have been a marksman in a previous life, she shot the other gang member in the same place…his bollocks. Now both men were rolling around the floor holding their wedding tackle, wailing in agony.

'Shit, sorry,' she said, grimacing at her handiwork.

She hurried from the living room to the bathroom, dreading what she might find. She discovered me slumped in the bath, I was tied up and gagged. I'd been beaten badly but I was still conscious.

'Mickey, fucking hell, what have they done to you,' she said, quickly untying me and helping me out of the bath. 'Are you ok, can you walk?'

'Just about,' I replied, glad to see a friendly face.

With Lisa's help I walked through the dining room, stepping over the two wounded gang members. I could not believe the state they were in.

'You shot them in the bollocks,' I said, shaking my head in disbelief.

'Yes, sorry about that, this gun has got a mind of its own,' she answered, holding it up.

'Don't point it at me, we don't want any more accidents,' I replied.

We left the apartment and we were soon in the car and out of there, leaving behind a small crowd that had formed in the street, probably because they had heard the shots from Lisa's pistol. Seconds later, looking in the rear-view mirror, I noticed we were being followed. I was about to tell Lisa what I had seen, but before I could say anything, she filled me in.

'It's ok, I know we're being followed. The police have been following me since I left Sali's. We need to head to the restaurant; they're probably staking that out too I expect.'

'What?'

'Trust me, I know what I'm doing, they won't be pulling anyone until the raid has taken place. It's all coordinated.'

Lisa was right, we arrived at the restaurant ten minutes later, took the bags out of the boot and walked straight through to the rear entrance and jumped in a fiat Punto, a vehicle that was kept there for anyone to use. Away we went, and this time we weren't followed. Brilliant, I mean who would use a fiat Punto as a getaway car?

'So, where to now?' Lisa asked.

'Just head north and keep going, we need to forget about everything, find somewhere miles away from anyone, somewhere we can relax and decide what to do with all of Sali's money,' I answered.

'It was never Sali's money. He got it through causing misery to thousands of people,' replied Lisa.

'How much was in the safe?'

'Enough to tide us over for a while! Probably around three hundred grand and some expensive jewellery and watches. You said forget about everything but what about Colin, haven't you got unfinished business?'

'Don't worry, the only person who should be worried about Colin, is Colin.'

Later that evening Colin was busy watching snooker on TV. He had been hiding out in his grandmother's house for the last few weeks. There was a knock on the door. Colin jumped up and headed for the back door, fearing it might be the Police.

'Who the fucking hell is that at this time?' Colin asked his grandmother.

The old woman peered through the net curtain.

'Relax son, it's a bloody salesman or a Jehovah's Witness. He came earlier, whilst you were out. They never know when to give up do they?'

'Move out of the way Gran, I'll soon sort him out,' said Colin, pushing up the sleeves of his jumper.

Colin threw the door open in a threatening manner.

'Look, why can't you lot just fuck off, we're not interested in whatever you're selling ok! Have you seen the time - its nearly nine o'clock for fuck's sake?'

'Oh no, I'm not trying to sell you anything Sir, I've come to give you something. It's from your good friend Mickey, my name is Yakubu.'

Yakubu held up a briefcase.

'Yakubu, hold on a minute why does that name ring a bell?' Colin asked. 'What is it?'

'Sir, I can't open it out here.'

Colin stood on the doorstep, looking totally puzzled.

'If I've come at the wrong time Mister Colin, we can rearrange,' said Yakubu.

Thinking that he might be missing out on something, Colin invited his unexpected guest into the house.

'No, you can come in, we might as well get it sorted now.'

They entered the living room, where Colin's grandmother was sitting watching the television.

'Gran, can you leave us alone for a few minutes while we discuss a little business?'

The old woman got up to leave the room.

'Let me know when you finish. Does the gentleman want a cup coffee?'

'That is a kind offer, thank you madam, but I never drink after 8pm.'

'Suit yourself,' she replied and shuffled out of the room.

'Sit down, what did you say your name was?' Colin asked.

'Yakubu Dimond, here's my card,' he replied, proffering a business card.

'Accountant?' Colin asked, looking at it.

'Yes, that is correct.'

'So, Yakubu, what is this all about and what's in your briefcase? I'm intrigued.'

Yakubu sat down and placed the briefcase on his knees, he pressed the two catches and it sprang open. He reached inside, pulled out a pistol and pointed it casually at Colin.

'Woah! Wait a minute, stop, we can talk about this?' Colin felt his stomach clenching. He knew he was in real danger.

'This is a Beretta Model 87, .22 calibre pistol with a sound suppressor attached, it's not my weapon of choice, but it's adequate for this job.'

'What do you mean for this job? I don't understand.'

Colin could not believe just how stupid he had been by letting this man into the house.

'You said Mickey sent you, listen, whatever Mickey is paying you, I'll double it, just put the fucking gun down, please,' he pleaded.

'I couldn't possibly do that, I'm loyal to all my clients, and anyway, Mickey didn't pay me, you did Mister Colin. You paid for your own contract killing.'

'Yakubu, now I remember the name, it was you I sent the money to.'

'Correct Mister Colin and you are lucky because I usually charge a lot more than you paid, but you see, I wanted this contract. I know that once you are dead my good friend, Mickey will have his closure and his revenge on the person who murdered his girlfriend.'

'I didn't mean to kill her, wrong place, wrong time.'

Yakubu fired the first shot, which hit Colin in the stomach. The second shot hit Colin in the eye followed by three more shots in rapid succession.

'Right place, right time Mister Colin.'

Yakubu closed the briefcase, stood up and retrieved his business card from the floor where it had fallen from Colin's lifeless hand. Placing it in his pocket, he crossed the room and turned off the light before leaving the room and walking out of the front door and into the night.

Epilogue

The sting by the Police and NCA was successful, five hundred Kilos of cocaine was confiscated with a street value of twenty million pounds and one of the country's largest coordinated drug operations had been broken up, following a series of raids up and down the country. Thirteen men, aged between twenty-four and fifty-nine, were apprehended during the raids. Between them, police say they were responsible for importing huge amounts of drugs into the UK from the Netherlands and Spain. The thirteen individuals were jailed for a total of 176 years.

In Spain, Sali was sitting in a popular bar which was often frequented by the local drug gangs, he was celebrating the success of another drugs shipment, completely oblivious to what had happened to his little empire back in the UK, when he received picture messages from his now ex-girlfriend Lisa. His expression changed from all smiles to rage when he saw the pictures of Filip, lying naked and spread-eagled on his bed and his empty safe. The pictures were followed by a text message.

Having a great time, hope you are too. Lisa and Mickey xxx

He slammed the phone down hard on the table in anger, cursing them under his breath and vowing to get his revenge on them both.

'What is it, Sali?' asked his supplier.

Sali did not get the opportunity to reply. His situation had just got a whole lot worse. Sali and his associates were surrounded by the Spanish Police.

Printed in Dunstable, United Kingdom